Ken Catran is an author of television/teenage fiction. His five writing awards include Ned Kelly Crime Writing and Young Adult Fiction 2002.

Other books by Ken Catran

Young Adult Fiction
Bloody Liggie

RISING

KEN CATRAN

UQP

First published 2004 by University of Queensland Press
Box 6042, St Lucia, Queensland 4067 Australia

www.uqp.uq.edu.au

© Ken Catran 2004

This book is copyright. Except for private study, research,
criticism or reviews, as permitted under the Copyright Act,
no part of this book may be reproduced, stored in a retrieval system,
or transmitted in any form or by any means without prior
written permission. Enquiries should be made to the publisher.

Typeset by University of Queensland Press
Printed in Australia by McPherson's Printing Group

Distributed in the USA and Canada by
International Specialized Book Services, Inc.,
5824 N.E. Hassalo Street, Portland, Oregon 97213–3640

Cataloguing in Publication Data
National Library of Australia

Catran, Ken.
  Protus rising.

  I. Title.

NZ823.2

ISBN 0 7022 3442 7

To Peter Reid, Astronomer. Who first roused my interest in the heavens.

Protus Intacta, Protus Intacta,
In Jupiter's red ocean, a new living factor.
Protus is free to live by its choice,
Freer than us, we have no voice.

We can create, give life, go beyond the pale,
So why do we die and why do we fail?
We explore other planets but let our world die.
I wonder if Protus can answer me why?

Ciardh Sonnaway
7 District, South Quadrant. 8634

PROLOGUE

I'd come awake from deep-frozen sleep before, but never with such an oppressive sense of bad dreams and murder. Of black nightmare and something very wrong. As though my instincts were already warning me.

Yes, weird and scary. But I'd never done such a long journey before in cryo-sleep. Nobody had, except our crew. Thinking that, letting my super-relaxed body get the message that my brain was active again. That the flight was over.

Over! Nearing Jupiter — the first humans to see it up close.

I can shift a little now. Yes, my body will have prepared for this over the last few weeks, support systems moving my arms and legs as I lay asleep, the cryogenic freezing gas being replaced with clean air. Space control had said we'd experience euphoria, and warned us against sudden movement. They hadn't warned us about this lingering sense of foreboding.

So I lie still in the bunk, look up at the control readouts overhead. Life system unhooked, cabin temperature normal. I look at the mirror they'd so thoughtfully put there. I'm twenty but feel older — maybe the sleep of the dead does that. Hair at shoulder-length, raising one unsteady hand to see long nails. So the medication controlling their growth had worked.

Clip your nails, says my slow-moving mind. Then, suddenly, What the hell — *Jupiter is outside!*

Forget the warnings, forget everything, this moment is too strong. I sit up on the side of the bunk, giddy for a minute, and slip on the utility-suit, my hands oddly heavy as I do up the zip. Next the boots and I set their magnetic sole-circuits for normal walking.

I stand up, another giddy spell, just for seconds this time. Nine months weightless but no ill effects. So the drugs controlling kidney function and bone-calcium loss have worked. Of course, if they hadn't, I'd be dead. I walk to the door and shakily push it open.

Now I'm outside, moving unsteadily, but moving. Past the other cabin doors. Commander Reliant's readout is still displayed, and so is Shanto's. This is puzzling — they should be downlined like mine. Elissa, hers *is* downlined, upstaging us yet again — she's always got to be first.

Not this time. I make the heavy boots move faster, thinking that Reliant and Shanto should be at the flight-deck too. I stop at the entrance, my boots clanging. And that bad-dream oppression floods back, because I don't believe what I'm seeing.

On the flight-deck is something out of a nightmare — a utility-suit, floating in a half-twist, one metal-soled boot still firmly on the deck, as though it were caught in a strange weightless death-dance. A name black-lettered on the suit.

DECLAN TULROPPER. My name.

There is nobody on the flight-deck. No sign of life. And

there's no way my spacesuit should be there. The nightmare gets worse as I lift my sleep-heavy eyes to the observation ports. Ahead of the ship is something I should not be seeing — something that mocks me by just being there. A voice penetrates suddenly through the system control.

'Declan, are you on the flight-deck?' This voice is firm, untouched by nightmare.

'Yes. Come up!'

I desperately make myself think, because there *has* to be a rational explanation — this could not be happening! But the flight-deck readouts say it is — they *have* to be wrong. I hear the sound of boots coming down the corridor. Elissa clangs in and stops as she sees the utility-suit.

'What —'

'Look outside.'

She looks for a very long moment then breathes my thoughts aloud. 'That isn't possible.'

She comes up slowly to stand beside me. Her bronze-black hair is cut untidily short, fingernails hastily clipped. Her face is frozen and her lips are moving again but she does not speak. She looks down at the readouts as I had, then up again through the observation port, where that pale mocking hangs in blackness.

'Our moon …', saying the words but not believing them. 'Our own moon. *Earth's moon.*'

'We are ten thousand kilometres on course to orbit.' Those are my words but I also do not believe them, my voice catching, that headless death-dancing spacesuit flopping beside me. 'Check fuel and resource levels.'

She does, with a small bewildered cry, stabbing queries into the console, but they come up the same. She shakes her head, maybe tingling with the same horror that I feel. 'It's like ... we've —'

'Right. Like we've been to Jupiter and back.'

'With no memory of it!'

Elissa sinks into her console chair as though suddenly heavy and tired. I sit down in mine. She looks at me, her eyes blank with horror, then stabs her console again. 'Shanto, Commander Reliant, report status. Are you out of cryo yet?'

The readouts flicker, and she turns to me with another blank look. 'Declan, their cryo-systems are locked. What the hell is happening!'

'Somehow we've completed our mission.' My words sound stupid, clunking like boots on the flight-deck. 'If we have, then —'

And the same thought hits Elissa. '*If* we have,' she snaps, inputting quickly.

She passes a hand through her hair as she looks at the readout. I don't have to see it. That blank look of horror is back in her eyes and she gives a puzzled headshake.

Now she accesses the ship's log, reading the lines of data, speaking them aloud in a low voice. 'According to this, we were in Jupiter orbit for four days, released the relay probe and Protus, all crew units activated —'

She breaks off. It is impossible, unreal and chilling. Nine months in cryo-sleep to Jupiter, four days awake in orbit. Four full days of ground-breaking — space-breaking — importance. Just about the most incredible journey ever made. And Protus, the most incredible thing ever made, launched on its mission. Then another nine-month flight home. And we could remember none of it.

Was it total amnesia induced by cryo-sleep? Surely not.

I'm struggling to think, and then I notice something I should have noticed earlier. Taped to one side of my console is a little triangular disc, one word printed boldly across it: PROTUS.

I pull the disc free. I know that printing — I slant T's upwards that way. At some time in those blank four days orbiting Jupiter, I had left this note to myself. There's a hollow feeling in my stomach, bad as a nightmare. I slot the disc into the console.

'Protus.' There's an almost-soundless hum as the password activates the disc. Elissa looks over from her console. 'All the other systems are still locked.'

'They're supposed to be.'

I don't know what makes me say that. It was like I was keying in to something — but without knowing what. Nine months ago in Jupiter-orbit I had locked all systems and left this disc for myself to find. Did I know that I would lose my memory? All at once I was scared that I was about to find out something I might not want to know.

'Go on,' Elissa whispered, sounding as scared as me.

'Protus disc, relay message.'

There's another hum and the console flickers, and a flat onscreen image appears. It's my own image, my own face and shorter hair. That chill comes over me again, and not just because I'm looking at myself, with no memory. Beside this onscreen-Declan was a side-port, and through the port could be seen the unmistakeable red glare of a huge planet mass.

Jupiter.

And something awesome had happened on Jupiter. Onscreen-Declan looked pale, exhausted, the eyes set with a haunting despair. A long cut down one side of the face was running blood. I put my hand to my own cheek. It was smooth, not even the trace of a scar.

'It's you,' breathes Elissa, then pauses, 'but it's not you.'

I knew what she meant. Onscreen-Declan had been through something terrible. It came out in the faltering way he began speaking. As though my voice was uttered through the lips of a stranger.

'Greetings from orbit off Callisto moon, Declan. I, your other self, leave this voice-ac log for you and Elissa.'

'Other self?' mutters Elissa.

Onscreen-Declan stops speaking a moment, breathing heavily. His cheeks are pale and he has dark smudges under his eyes. *'Yes, your other self. You will have no memory of this when you wake up. For a very good reason. But I must tell you.'*

I was rigid now and so was Elissa. That tired voice, with its ghastly mix of mockery and despair, was compelling. Still, I can't shake off the impression that it's not my face.

'We released Protus, maybe the best thing, maybe the worst thing we ever did. Nothing will be the same. The whole damn solar system will change ...'

What is he talking about? There's another pause as onscreen-Declan takes some blue-green capsules, the protein medication we use on deep-space voyages to counter long-term weightlessness. But six of them? One a month is enough. Six means that he must have massive internal problems, but I feel fine. He gulps the pills with some water and leans back, giving that haunted, mocking smile again.

'Better start at the beginning, when I woke up from cryo-sleep ...'

He swallows more water. We are looking at him, at the observation port behind him, at that huge red mass bathing the control deck in red-tinted light. Jupiter, the planet where Protus had gone. And now the solar system will change.

Onscreen-Declan sits up, seeming less tired. Maybe the medication helped. His voice is less shaky but still filled with horror.

'When I woke up from cryo not knowing where I was. Or who I was. Everything was blank. I wish to hell it had stayed that way.'

ONE

> *And you pause again, onscreen-Declan, because nightmare is flooding back into your voice and you have to find the words to speak. You are like a drowning man in raging waters, having to keep your head up and breathe. That first hour when things were nearly normal, except that you didn't know who you were or where you were ...*

FIRST VIS REC TRANSMISSION BEGINS: I came awake in a strange steel room, unable to move. I could feel my body, my arms and legs, but they were soft and limp. And I did not know who I was, or where I was.

Somehow that didn't matter — like it was a problem resolved. Maybe with no memory nothing mattered. I was sitting in a big high-backed chair and facing me was a lengthways-shuttered screen. A bank of four consoles and three other high-backed chairs. I was breathing from a dry throat, my neck stiff as though I hadn't moved my head for a long time. Something brushed my neck — my own long hair. I heard my vertebrae snick and crack as I inclined my clumsy head to look down at the console keyboard and a scrap of blue paper stuck between the keys. Movement trickled through my body now, like a spiky little river; one hand, encased in a silver glove, was moving. I could make the fingers waggle and the silver hand move.

That scrap of blue paper seemed to fascinate me and I moved my hand towards it, aware, as feeling flowed through my body, that tight straps were holding me to the chair. I flicked the scrap of blue paper with my silver fingers and the first strange thing happened.

The paper floated into the air.

It was not flicked up, it just floated. My silver fingers reached to grab it but that flick must have activated the controls. Ahead, there was a jarring suddenness and the shutters rolled back like a long steel eyelid. They were covering a forward observation port and through it came a picture too stunning for words.

There was a darkness that was total and black, and ahead was a perfectly round planetoid, pitted with so many dark-grey ice-craters that they overlapped each other. The planetoid reflected red on one side, because beyond it hung the curved edge of a larger mass, flashing orange and red. Beautiful sharp patterns of colour cut into that blackness — and still I did not know myself; or what I was looking at.

In this blank innocence I wondered why that blue paper floated in the air, and why there were straps holding me. I was not afraid, even when another silver-gloved hand appeared beside my face. Touching my shoulder, someone slipped into the chair beside me.

'Jupiter ...' breathed this second person.

The word was somewhere between a sigh and a statement. From the faraway blankness of my mind I wondered where she had come from. She looked at me as though I should know her long face, her brown eyes and her bronze-black shoulder-length hair.

'Chewing-gum wrapper,' she whispered, smiling at me. 'I put it there nine months ago.' Now a large corner of the orange mass came into view. 'Declan, how do you feel?'

Declan? It meant nothing. I was as puzzled and trapped as a helpless child and less understanding. This was a strange dream going nowhere. The young woman did not seem to notice my confusion as she leaned forward to check her console. Her fingernails were untidily clipped, I noticed.

'Commander Reliant and Shanto are out of cryo,' she said. Then she became aware that I was still looking at her. 'Declan, are you still spaced out on cryo-gas?'

'Reliant and Shanto ...' Echoing the names. No, just words. The young woman accesses her readouts. 'They should be out by now.' Then she frowns, jabbing at her console. 'I hope they're not messing with Protus —'

Protus!

That word jabbed painfully through my brain like voltage. *Protus!* Like sunlight splitting apart the blankness, a vivid deep-life pattern flooded.

Protus. I was Declan Tulropper, co-pilot; she of the short hair and untidily clipped fingernails was Elissa Jinglesaw, science officer. I was nearly twenty, top of my intense and competitive class, the best of the best. Forget Columbus discovering America, forget the moon-landing. This was deep space, Jupiter, the most important voyage that humans had ever made.

So why did I forget? Well, I forgot that loss of memory was a trivial side-effect of cryo. But the tip of the iceberg was about to erupt like a flaming volcano. I was already in Declan-mode, full of drive and command before Reliant came up, giving orders.

'OLLIE, full systems check.' OLLIE, Operational Liaison Link Internal Extramural, state-of-the-art voice-activation for *Copernicus*, the greatest space-cruiser ever built. 'OLLIE, online!'

Nothing. The designer deep-space voice-ac systems that would let a five-year-old fly a spaceship (not that any would get a chance to) had gone suddenly dumb. I shouted this time, although getting angry with voice-ac systems never works.

'OLLIE, online!'

Elissa shrugged. 'Shanto was programming right up to take-off; maybe it's still voice-acced to him. Or maybe to Commander Reliant.' She slapped a hand on my shoulder, even smiled. 'Declan, lighten up. We're here!'

Lighten up? I should be dancing, yelling for joy because the orange mass of planet Jupiter was filling our port. A huge orb, outlined with a nimbus of fire, layered orange and red. Now rotating, the giant Red Spot came into view, a baleful blood-dark eye.

Just seeing *that* up close! A storm-centre that was itself many times bigger than Earth — one of the many secrets of Jupiter that Protus would tell us about. Elissa was right, I should be doing cartwheels — and I could in this weightless air. We were explorers, seeing undreamed-of sights, so why did my feeling of disquiet continue?

'Elissa, we need OLLIE online. Get Shanto up here.'

'Shanto, on deck, there's a planet called Jupiter you might

care to look at.' She paused and looked at me. 'Commander Reliant?'

I nodded and Elissa paged the commander, but politely, because Reliant was a tough disciplinarian. Thirty years old, she was the best deep-space pilot on Spoke and she hadn't wanted such a young crew. But the Earth-plagues left her little choice.

There was no answer and my disquiet grew. She *would* answer. Hell, she should be here by now. And Shanto would answer, even make a joke. Elissa was concerned now, too.

'Shall I bring the others out of cryo?'

'No.' Something *was* wrong. I got up. My knees were still a bit weak but I could move alright. 'I'll do a personal check. Stay here.'

Elissa hesitated then nodded. Yes, I'd given her a direct order because the two senior officers were out of cryo and not answering. My space-boots were working fine and outside the control deck I walked faster, not caring that my hasty clopping would carry back to Elissa. *Wrong, wrong, something was wrong!*

Commander Reliant first. I thumbed the release and the cabin door slid open. Empty. Her cryo-systems were disconnected, the bed-straps dangling open. The photo of her partner was there, and the university netball pennant I'd seen her pin over the bunk before take-off. I had a strong sense of something out of place, then Elissa interrupted on the intercom.

'Anything?' Her voice was taut.

'Cabin empty.'

'Probably a simple explanation, Declan.'

A deep-space commander not responding to her page?

No, there was nothing simple about that. I told her to keep paging.

The next cabin was Shanto's. I took a step inside. Something swirled out at me and I stopped as though meeting a strange beast. It was water vapour and I could see what was on the bunk.

'Is he there?' Opening Shanto's door registered on Elissa's console.

'Yes.'

Shanto Santana, Lead Science Officer — my best friend on the Spoke Carthage orbit station, who knew all the right people and secured my place on this crew. Yes, he was still in his cabin.

He'd been about to get out of his bunk, cryo-systems disconnected, straps open. One leg and one arm were over the side and a wet trail ran down his arm from the dark patch in the centre of his chest. It reddened the water vapour around him. His eyes were closed, though his face wore its normal expression of placid mockery.

Elissa's voice again. 'Tell him to online OLLIE.'

'You'd better get down here. Quick!' I said.

Shanto was dead.

Elissa did come quickly. She even stepped into the floating mist of water by his bed, touched him, checked for a pulse. 'Body's still warm.' She shook her head and looked at me. 'Entry wound like a stab — right through the heart. Must've been immediate.' She touched something floating over the body. 'What's this?'

'His fruit knife.' A little ivory-handled thing, it was practically his good-luck charm. 'Too small for an entry wound like that.'

'Right.'

'There's no way this could've been an accident?'

'No,' she replied. 'Or suicide.' She looked at the tiny reddened droplets flashing prismatic colours like a rainbow dipped in blood. 'Where the hell does all this vapour come from?'

'Fluid from his cryo-system. Maybe a tube sprung while he was disconnecting,' I replied.

Or torn loose. A horrible picture came to mind — of Shanto waking, struggling to disconnect as his murderer approached. But if that was the case, why did he have such a calm look on his face? But this was no time to look for answers. We had to find Commander Reliant first.

'We can't do anything here,' said Elissa.

'No.'

There was no emotion in her voice and none in mine. We were still too numb with shock to feel anything. She flicked the little knife and it bobbed away. We backed out of the red mist into the corridor and I shut the door.

Both of us were thinking the same thing.

Our mission was two years in the planning. Spaceship *Copernicus*, two years in construction, in the massive Spoke assembly bays. We had allowed for cryo-effects; we had taken medication to prevent kidney failure and bone-calcium loss from a long-term weightless flight; we had screened our ship from solar radiation. And it had all worked.

Now Spaceship *Copernicus* was among the five outer moons of Jupiter. One of them, Callisto, was involved in the first part of our mission. Then would come the most important solar probe of the twenty-first century. And thirty minutes after wake-up, the Commander was missing and the Lead Science Officer dead.

'We'd better search the ship,' said Elissa. She even led the way back to the flight-deck. She was always bossy, even back on Spoke; it was time to show her who was in command.

I stopped at Commander Reliant's cabin and went inside to the arms locker. I tucked a hand-laser into my belt and Elissa, standing in the doorway, held out her hand for one. I just shut the locker and re-coded the lock.

She flushed, her eyes angry over her high cheekbones, and shouted, 'Do you suspect *me*?'

'Let's find Reliant,' I said.

She scowled angrily, but the pale shock was still on her face. We were in a nightmare and I sensed that more awful things lay ahead. And yes, my watching Declan, I was right. They did.

So we checked the cabins on visual-scan, each in turn. Simon, Belinda, Conception and Redgrove were all alive and in the last peaceful stage before coming awake. Their temperatures were down but that was the last remnants of cryo-gas leaving their bodies.

Copernicus was still turning and Callisto was becoming larger in our observation port. We had to begin our mission and we needed OLLIE online — now. We were back on the flight-deck and I was thinking hard.

Reliant *must* have the code-word as well as Shanto. *Copernicus* was the biggest spaceship ever built, but the layout was simple. Two decks, storage and cabin units, the engine-room. Nothing hidden and no secret places to hide. Easy to search and only one major item below-decks — Protus.

'Protus?' I asked. 'Could anything hide in its tank?' What I really meant was *Could anything be dumped there — as in Reliant's body?*

But Elissa — Second Science Officer — sprang to the defence of her shared creation.

'Impossible!' she snapped.

'We still have to look.'

We went down to the second deck. All the stores and equipment readouts showed that they had been locked since take-off. They were tightly stacked and a systems check showed no entry. At the end of the deck was a lab-room and side-cabin, with another figure under cryo: Simon, our ship's engineer.

Before us now, in its own sealed and massive tank, was the reason for our journey. A designer creation, the most incredible unit of biological engineering since the dawn of time.

Protus.

TWO

Even the experts could not agree on how alive Protus Intacta was — whether it lived as we do, or even as a fish did. It swam in a dark, cloudy red protein-fluid and, as though shy, avoided our gaze when we first opened the steel shutters over one glass wall of the tank. Not ordinary glass, of course, just as Protus was not ordinary life.

Shanto had said that nothing designed by him was ordinary.

'It survived the journey well,' said Elissa.

Protus had been 'swimming' in that fluid for nine months. It did not need sleep. But when our light appeared, it backed off with small powerful fin movements into the red murk. We could see only two luminous globes like glowing eyeballs on the end of strings. And the impression of bulky, graceful movement.

'He doesn't seem to like us,' I said.

'It,' she corrected. 'It has no gender. We didn't design a partner — it wouldn't have been fair since it has an infinite genetic lifespan.' She was inspecting readouts, checking seals. 'Nothing has been in or out since launch. You won't find Reliant in there, dead or alive.'

'Until we do find her, I'm in command,' I said.

'Of course, Commander.'

Protus swam closer as though interested in our words. Its sensory perceptions would pick up our sound waves vibrating off the glass. Beside me, Elissa went closer, her lips moving, as though calling it in. She and Shanto had spent months creating Protus. It came even closer and we could see the downward-pouting mouth, the long antennae on either side of the head.

She looked at me. 'What now, Commander?'

There was a slight pause before the last word, and it suddenly hit me. Yes, I was in command. The success of this important and costly mission was on my shoulders now. I led the way back up the ladder. (This was simple. Cut the magnetic pressure on my boots and kick up through zero gravity to the top deck.) Elissa followed and I reset the magnetic control.

We walked down the long central passage to the control deck. The firm clang-clang of our footsteps was the only real thing in this nightmare. We settled back in our control chairs.

'Even on a ship this size Reliant can't just vanish,' Elissa said quietly.

'Then we back-track readouts for the last twenty-four hours,' I replied. 'Longer, if we have to.'

'Without OLLIE it'll take all day ... Commander.'

Still the slight pause before that word. I nodded though, rubbing my hands over my face, still weak but not hungry or thirsty. Jupiter's red mass was closer and so was Callisto. I had to forget about Reliant for now. There were things I had to do.

'Wake up the other crew?' asked Elissa.

'Wake up OLLIE first,' I replied. We needed the password, and I remembered something. 'Shanto's personal disc, he always had it in a locket around his neck.'

I would rather have sealed that cabin and let Earth and Spoke sort out what happened. But I had to check. I opened the door and walked through the red mist to Shanto's body. I slipped my finger inside his tunic collar. His body was cold now.

'Anything?' Elissa's voice came on the intercom, as she watched from the monitor.

I made myself check his pockets then his personal locker. Cryo cabins were small and there was nowhere to hide anything. I shook my head, knowing she could see that on the monitor. Then I stepped back through the doorway, out of that red mist, and shut the door.

'Okay, seal the cabin — '

Just at that moment Elissa screamed loudly. The sound chilled me — Elissa was not easily frightened. Her voice gasped with pure shock through the intercom.

'Declan — the body!'

I thumbed the door open. There was the mist, the bunk — but no Shanto. I gaped, then walked back into that swirling water vapour.

'I only took my eyes off the screen for a moment,' said Elissa. She was already back in control. 'It just *vanished*!'

'Impossible!'

'Then where is it … Commander?'

Shanto's bunk was empty. The impression of his body still

remained and the water vapour still swirled, but now I noticed something else. The water vapour was no longer reddened, and even the droplets of Shanto's blood were gone, the rainbow washed clean.

This was not real, I told myself. This could not happen. But this was no illusion, no hallucinatory after-effect of cryo-sleep; it was something that I could not even begin to think about. All I did know was that Shanto's dead body was no longer there.

Gone without a trace.

I backed out. 'Seal the unit.'

The door slid shut, the systems hummed. Shanto was gone, but I had to put that forcibly out of my mind. Reliant had to be found.

'Stay monitoring, Elissa.'

Opening Reliant's cabin I had that sense, as I'd had before, of something out of place. I was registering now what I should have realised earlier. And should have checked at once.

'Seen something?' came Elissa's voice.

'Yes.'

I flipped up the lid of an inset locker beside Reliant's bunk. Empty. So even if we did not know what had happened to Shanto's body, we had a clue about Reliant. Elissa had seen it on the monitor, so there was no need to tell her what to do.

'Coming back on deck,' I said and shut the door behind me.

She was already inputting when I got there. Reliant's inset locker held her spacesuit, which was now missing. Each crew-member had their own ID locating code. The signal begins working as soon as the suit is put on. Elissa brought up the code. 'Active-active-active,' it said, because Reliant had put on her spacesuit and gone out of the ship.

'Signals begin at starboard airlock,' said Elissa quietly.

'Access hull monitors on starboard side.'

OLLIE would have done it at once. Elissa took half a minute using the manual program. All the time I was thinking, *This is impossible!* Reliant was a tough veteran, the ace flight-commander on Spoke. She would *never* leave the spaceship like this.

Elissa's face was white, one hand clenched tight as the outer hull came up onscreen. All those thousands of tiny overlapping plates that made up the hull's white outer skin were now flickering red with Jupiter-light as Elissa moved the surveillance around.

And now we could see the big outflung tail-fins and the large coil of the engine that had brought us across space at hundreds of thousands of kilometres per hour. No spaceship could travel faster than ours, even with the weight of our payload. And there would be no second chance with this mission.

'Oh hell,' whispered Elissa.

My mind echoed the words, though I didn't say them aloud. Before us was something we did not want to see.

A spacesuit figure stood motionless on the hull, the magnetic-soled boots firmly planted, arms to the sides, facing away from us.

'Cut to the end surveillance unit, I said quietly.

Elissa hissed, as though anticipating tragedy. She brought up the hull visuals set in the tail-fin. Now we could see the front of the figure.

There were no answers to our problems there. Just more

questions as horrible and puzzling as those inside the ship. That red Jupiter-light on the spacesuit-figure should have flashed most strongly on the visored helmet-head. It did not, because the visor was up, rolled back into the dome of the helmet. Only a black oval was visible.

'Enhance to one metre,' I said, knowing even then what we would find.

The distance closed and Elissa gave that little indrawn hiss of horror and distress again.

There was no face inside the helmet. The suit was empty. There was still no sign of Reliant, but at least now we knew why. And where she was: on her way to Jupiter.

Somehow, out there, her visor must have opened. Her body would have been sucked out in one appalling moment. Now her imploded remains were somewhere in a decreasing orbit behind us.

'What would she be doing out there on the hull?' Elissa's voice shook. 'And spacesuits just *don't* malfunction like that.'

And what force could have torn the body loose from the inert hull gravity? No time to think about it now. 'Let's get the crew out of cryo,' I said.

Elissa nodded and opened the program on her console. I leaned back and shut my eyes as Commander Reliant's voice sounded through the control room: her comments on each crew-member were voice-acced to their wake-up; they were clinical and terse, like her.

REDGROVE SINAPHOLE: 'Ambition and deceit in equal proportions, good at his work but not a good person.'

Yes, my thoughts too about Redgrove.

CONCEPTION IMODA: 'Good expertise but highly strung; lacks commitment, I think.'

BELINDA HEDON: 'Intelligent, reliable, but another of these young people who are all brains and no perception.'

SIMON MARSUPLIO: 'Perceptive, but too focused on his work.'

Then Elissa, who was 'dedicated, trustworthy, not easily fooled'. Elissa smiled when she heard this. And me? 'Competent and solid, but too trusting and lacks judgment.' In other words, I liked Shanto and she didn't. Last came Reliant's description of him:

SHANTO SANTANA: 'Sociopath, totally self-centred, thinks the solar system was created for his personal benefit. Untrustworthy.'

Well, I said she didn't like him.

And now she was gone and I was in command. The success of this mission lay on my shoulders and the two people who knew most about it were dead. An undreamed-of opportunity, you might think. Get this right and I would have a ticket to anywhere.

But my dreams of this mission had become nightmares.

Elissa had finished inputting the wake-up codes. Even now the others would be opening their eyes, and in half an hour or so would be on the flight-deck with us, wanting the same kind of answers as we did, about Shanto and Commander Reliant.

'Let's get that spacesuit back in here and check it out.'

Elissa bought up Reliant's code and waited as the flickering lines of data came onscreen. She shook her head. 'There's some kind of override. It won't move.'

Another line of data came onscreen. Elissa simply pointed to it without speaking.

Our spacesuits are state-of-the-art. Mini-circuits in the fabric and boots create a second, intelligent layer of skin and muscle. If the person inside has an accident, the suit — by remote control — can be walked back to the airlock. And there, onscreen, like a death-warrant, was an instruction to override the suit's safety systems and open the visor. Whoever did that knew exactly what would happen to Reliant.

This was our second murder.

THREE

> *What is that word? Doppelgänger. The apparitional double of a living person. That's how onscreen-Declan seems to me, but he's more than that. He knows terrible things and grins at us like the whole solar system is a black joke. Croaking as though it's hard to believe, then coughs, and goes on.*

'Reliant comes out of cryo early, she kills Shanto and takes a walk outside. So who overrides *her* suit systems?'

That was Conception. Tall and dark-skinned, she had short black hair and wide brown eyes that looked candid but hid a nervous intensity. Even after nine months' cryo-sleep she was twitchy.

'Or Shanto kills her then somehow kills himself in a state of remorse.' This was from Redgrove, also tall and sharp-faced, with red-brown hair and a little pointed moustache. Even on emergency wake-up he'd trimmed himself neatly before coming out. His eyebrows were plucked and as sharp as the antennae of insects. 'Of course, I can't imagine Shanto suffering remorse, can you, Declan?'

'Commander, if you don't mind.' No first-name terms when you are in command. Redgrove knew that and was needling me. He leaned against the bulkhead as though bored. His dark green eyes rested lazily on me.

'Excuse me, Commander, there are other possibilities. Somebody programmed to wake early from cryo' — Simon, thin and pale with blue eyes and long fair hair, wanting to get this over with so he could get back to his precious engines — 'kills them and goes back under cryo.'

'Surely the Commander's checked that,' said Redgrove, a little too smoothly, meaning: *Has anyone checked Declan's readouts?*

'If somebody wanted to spike this mission, they'd have to do more than that,' said Belinda. She was a thickset woman with a blunt, direct manner, a strong square face and a close-fitting skullcap of black curls — a geologist and planet environment specialist.

'A ... stoner?' asked Simon nervously.

Redgrove just hooted and even serious Belinda rolled her eyes. Stoners, as in 'stone-age', were the latest version of eco-terrorists. They aimed to destroy everything high-tech and become one with nature again. No, stoners were fanatics. They would have gone on smashing — and killing.

'Readouts will confirm wake-up,' said Elissa.

'Readouts can be altered,' muttered Conception, hugging herself tightly.

'OLLIE's program was set on Spoke,' snapped Elissa. 'Nobody on the ship can change it, not even — '

She was about to say 'not even Shanto' and Shanto was

dead. We were going around in circles and all the time Callisto moon and the first part of our mission were getting closer. It was time to start acting like a commander.

'I'm logging all this then leaving it, okay? We have the mission to complete.'

'Surely, Commander,' Redgrove said, very smoothly — too damn smoothly. He'd wanted my job on Spoke and had done his underhand best to get it. He hated the idea of my being in command and would stick the knife in whenever he could. And he and Conception were good friends. I'd have to watch her too.

'Stations everyone,' I said. 'Callisto coming up. We have one chance at this.'

I nearly said 'That's an order', but Reliant never had to. So I looked at them and one by one — Redgrove last — they filed out. Elissa slipped into her console chair and brought up the Callisto program.

'I've done the best systems check I could without OLLIE. Related energy consumption and oxygen levels, and I've scanned every corner I could. There's nothing on board but us — and Protus.'

I didn't believe in a killer stowaway. But there was one other option, and Elissa would know that too. An option that was pure speculation right now.

We had pushed further into space than any manned craft before us. Past Mars and the manned outpost there. This close to Jupiter, we were on the shores of an unknown land. We could scan for anything Earth-known. But we had no way of checking for something that was totally unlike anything we knew, something from that unknown land.

Something alien.

* * *

I had always been fascinated with planet Jupiter, the biggest planet in our solar system, maybe as big as they get anywhere. It is huge beyond comprehension, with a massive gravity. It plays backstop and pulls in a lot of comets and asteroids that would otherwise hit Earth. Just a few years ago it sucked up a comet big enough to shatter our planet, and barely hiccuped.

And this big red giant has sixty-plus moons by the latest count. I did a thesis on the 'Galilean' moons that put me on the fast-track to Spoke Carthage, just before the first viral plague hit Earth. I knew their histories as well as I knew my own. Studying them was like studying the evolution of our solar system in miniature.

Tiny Almathea is the closest to Jupiter, red in colour and irregularly shaped. Next are the 'Galilean' moons, named after their discoverer, the astronomer Galileo. All are locked in a tidal tug of war with the largest, Europa.

We could see Europa now, on the forward scanner. It was magic to be this close. Europa was smooth and light-coloured, criss-crossed by long dark lines. Then would come Io, still being reworked by sulphur volcanos, the way Earth once was. Then Ganymede, the largest moon, heavily cratered and cut with channels running for hundreds of kilometres.

All of them with incredible secrets still to be unlocked.

'Callisto coming up,' said Elissa, unable to keep a touch of excitement from her voice.

Callisto. Moon number five. The furthest out and multi-cratered. I was cold, with an icy wriggling tension, because this *had* to work. If not, we could turn around and go home. Blast Redgrove, he should have reported by now.

Hell and damn! Even now he's playing his little power games, wants me to shout down the intercom, show my panic. No, Redgrove, this ball is in your court. So I sat there and let my face go deadpan, aware that Elissa was looking at me, her mouth framing a question, because Callisto was filling our observation ports. Alright, Redgrove, you cocky jerk, I won't play your stupid game. My hand moved to the intercom —

There was a buzz and then Redgrove's impersonal voice: 'Relay is ready.'

He and Conception were in the second control bay. Simon and Belinda were in the rear control unit by the engines. Callisto was filling our ports, big, round and dirty grey, with spots of fresh ice from a recent meteor strike.

'Release!' I said.

And nothing happened on the screen readouts — nothing!

Redgrove came back on the intercom. 'No release showing.'

And Simon, tense as hell. 'Systems failure.'

'Try again,' I snapped.

Elissa opened the intercom. We could hear the click-click, and a mutter from Conception.

An edge of panic had crept into Redgrove's voice. 'The probe won't release — malfunction!'

Oh hell, we had thirty seconds then we'd be out of range. 'Simon, check the circuit links.'

'They are working.' His voice was shrill but steady. 'It just won't release.'

With OLLIE, we could have stopped *Copernicus*, checked for the fault, and orbited Callisto for another run. But we had this single pre-programmed run and twenty seconds left, fifteen seconds —

Take a deep breath, Declan, I told myself. Keep your voice steady and firm. 'Simon, that bloody thing has to release. Or Protus won't have the boost power for Earth transmission —'

Suddenly there was a loud humming click. The release code flickered onscreen. From below our hull a huge four-winged insect-like machine shot out, angling down to the pitted light-dark surface of Callisto.

The last seconds flickered to zero. That was too, too close.

'On course, all systems functioning,' came Simon's voice.

'The malfunction just somehow cleared itself.' Conception gave a nervous laugh. 'Must have heard you swearing.'

'Secure,' I said.

The probe had already disappeared. It would land, upend itself and dig into the planetoid surface with its drill-sting tail. Almost completely under cover, it would be safe from meteor-strike. When Protus began sending data, the probe would boost it to Earth.

If we could get Protus to Jupiter.

'Well done, Commander,' said Elissa.

I just nodded. I couldn't even smile. We had got it right despite ourselves. Elissa knew that but it was nice to hear those words. Had we not succeeded, I would have made an A-grade scapegoat.

Simon's voice came on the intercom. 'Relay in place, operational.' A pause, then, 'Good work. I would never have dared make that decision.'

I smiled this time. Redgrove would have heard that and

he'd be boiling. But forget him. This wasn't a contest of personalities. In about twelve hours time the big decision would have to be made — whether to release Protus.

'I'll need a program to reduce our orbit, Elissa. Get us closer.'

Before even thinking about release, we had to somehow coax the massive bulk of *Copernicus* into a lower orbit, with no help from the voice-ac flight systems. It was theoretically possible. Theoretically.

'Elissa has control,' I said into the intercom. 'Everyone else stand down and go to cabin units. Intercom open at all times, no exit without clearance from me.'

Of course Redgrove was first to break the silence. 'Are we under restriction?' he asked sharply.

'No, Redgrove, you're obeying orders.' Then I remembered something else. 'Simon, we'll patch the ship's design through to your cabin. I want another intensive scan of the ship's interior, metre by metre. Check for anything abnormal. Anything.'

He acknowledged, but the others did not break the silence; maybe they were sulking about being pushed around, but who cared. We were on course and there were things I had to do.

'I'll be in my unit, Elissa.'

The other doors were already shut and the system's light was on over each one. One hour out of cryo-sleep and the ship was a prison. I tried to voice-ac my door open and then remembered that the voice-ac wasn't working. Voice-ac is sometimes like breathing — you only notice it when it stops.

I entered the cabin. 'Cabin' was another old-fashioned Earth-term, like 'deck' or 'bulkhead'. I sat on the narrow bed and the airbase squeaked; it was programmed to keep my body moving and my muscles toned during the long flight. The only other furniture was a console, a personal-effects locker and a bigger one for the spacesuit. I still had the hand-laser and I pulled it out, checked the safety catch and let it bob away in the air. It reminded me of Shanto's fruit-knife — was that floating around during his nine months of cryo? Then I remembered my cryo-control read-outs, which would have registered on my console. All they'd show was whether I snored. I had another thought — perhaps I walked in my sleep.

This didn't seem likely, but there was no harm in making sure. I opened the console and there flicked a bold line of data: 'READ DISCS WHEN YOU'RE OUT OF CRYO. CODED, BUT YOU KNOW WHAT WE'RE ALL ABOUT, DON'T YOU?' It was signed SHANTO and that was vintage Shanto. It might be an important message but he still had to tease. Giving me the code would have been too easy. And thinking about him, I wished he was here now.

'Shanto, you're still a joker.'

'Copy that, Commander?' came Elissa's startled voice. Of course, intercom to the flight-deck was open.

'Thinking aloud,' I said. If Shanto had secrets, I wanted to be the first to know them.

Anyway, Shanto's code was easy enough. *You're not as silly as you look, Declan,* he would say. We were all about our mission and our mission was the release of Protus. In my locker was a set of four numbered voice-ac discs. I slipped the first into the activate slot.

'Protus.'

There was a little humming click. Then the hologram-receiving points in the far corner flickered and shimmered into life.

A tall young man stood — lounged — there, with all the solid reality of hologram life. In his late teens, he had a clean-shaven head and a thin sharp face, and a wide humorous mouth that made him look as if he thought the world was a joke. He wore a faded blue utility-suit with one gold bar lopsided on the collar. He flapped a lazy hand at me.

'Hi, Declan.' This was Shanto as I remembered him, not with the quiet death-lines of sleep on his face. 'I'll be busy with Protus when you wake up. Take control. I'll handle Reliant and brief you on the control deck. Oh, by the way, OLLIE's personalised to me.' He circled with one long finger. 'Something suitably Jovian.'

Then he stood up straight and pointed at me. The mocking tone was gone from his voice. 'Smarten up, Declan, and stay cool. We are onto something very big.'

The hologram shimmered and disappeared. I was looking at the empty corner and all I had were more questions. Shanto would handle Reliant? The casual way he said that. Maybe she 'handled' Shanto first. She was tough enough. And Shanto *had* locked the voice-ac systems — *that* code-word would be less obvious.

I knew one thing, though. Shanto had not gone straight into cryo like the rest of us. He had spent months reprogramming the ship's computers. He had hijacked the whole mission, but I could not think of a single reason why.

FOUR

> *Good work with that probe, my onscreen doppelgänger. Driving a spaceship on manual is not easy. You did it — I did it. Hell, this is crazy, I have no memory of something so awesome. And the things you haven't talked about so far, the plague, family, Shanto. Each in turn, yes, that's how I'd do it — and you know how your listener responds. Elissa listening to this too, as blank as me. And as tense as me. Because I sense there's a lot more to come. And none of it good.*

I could not think of a single reason why Shanto would do this. Power for power's sake? No, he wasn't into that. We'd been planning this mission since that first automatic probe returned from circling Jupiter. So, there was something in the background that I'd missed. Something on Spoke Carthage.

Spoke. Any clues there? Six Spokes orbited Earth. They were called that because corridors and an outer circle radiated from an inner hub like a giant spoked wheel. They had science laboratories, building bays, processing units for food (basic and dull), water from ice-meteors and recycled oxygen, and were self-sufficient like the old city-states they were named after: Carthage, Copan, Nara, Rhodes and so on. After my training was completed, I stayed on Carthage: 'retention due to pandemic on Earth'.

Pandemic. A cute name for a quick-acting deadly virus that turned your saliva green before killing you — cuter than 'Greenspit'. Fifty per cent of Earth's population died — a number too big to comprehend. So the shuttle-lines were cut and that meant quick promotion.

There were no clues in the pre-mission data either. A memo from Reliant e-mailed to my diary said that the pandemic would make the Spokes even more independent. Was there something there? Now my readouts were showing a personal message, telecast before take-off. It must have come when I was halfway into cryo.

There's a photo, an Earth-scene. I knew that little patio and the high trellis covered with honeysuckle. The barbeque, food and drink on a side-table. Four people posing, my mother with her big proud smile. My father with a burned sausage on his fork. Ciardh, my girlfriend, not smiling, her blue hair gathered in plaits. And me, grinning, pulling a face, in a black T-shirt with zigzag yellow stripes and baggy purple shorts, on a high because I was fifteen and Spoke-bound, and the whole universe was mine.

A sound-bite was attached: Ciardh's voice, tense, trying not to sound unhappy. 'Hello, Declan. I found this the other day. Hope it makes you smile. Have to keep this short, as the telecast is being interrupted by the plague.'

Her voice hesitated, as though all this was an impulse. She

sounded uncertain, collecting her thoughts. 'Declan, Greenspit's reached our city. I wasn't sure I should tell you, but you have the right to know. Our sector's quarantined, so we'll be okay, Dad says. Declan, you're a pain half the time but I'm so proud of you going to Jupiter. You say there are answers to Earth's problems. Well, how can we make something like Protus and still be in such a mess? I'm not a Stoner but — well, I wrote this poem.'

Her voice was still as tense as that unsmiling image. I'd joked about her hair, said it made her look like a long skinny bluebell. Her voice spoke the words clearly, with force.

> *Protus Intacta, Protus Intacta,*
> *In Jupiter's red ocean, a new living factor.*
> *Protus set free to live by its choice,*
> *Freer than us, we have no voice.*
>
> *We can create, give life, go beyond the pale,*
> *So why do we die and why do we fail?*
> *We explore other planets but let our world die.*
> *I wonder if Protus can answer me why?*

'Declan, cloning, genetics ... where's the value of being human? Oh, you'd just prattle about Shanto and how he thinks we can solve everything with science. Well, we haven't yet and nearly half the world is dead. I want to be human, I want you so much, because with the plague coming —'

I hit the cut-off button. I knew why Ciardh sent me this. She was in quarantine, but she knew the end was coming.

Yes, I cut it off — because I was the commander and that came first. I had a downlined system, locked to a password in Shanto's dead brain. I pulled off my boots and let myself float upwards over the bunk. Being weightless helped me think. And I had a lot to think about.

Such as reading the unreadable mind of Shanto Santana. So, first — sum up the facts.

Shanto, dead and missing. He'd hijacked the most important space-mission ever and he never did anything by halves. In a few hours we would have to manually fly *Copernicus* up against the deadly, grabbing hold of Jupiter's gravity.

I need Shanto's code-word!

There was one — he'd hinted as much — and he'd used it to place the flight under his total control. I eased myself into a cross-legged pose above the bunk. Shanto did nothing simply; there were always the subtle underlays of his deep thinking. His password would reflect that, and our mission. Something suitably Jovian, he'd said.

I thought for three long hours, aware that every minute brought us closer to Jupiter, and that Elissa was alone on the flight-deck. I checked with her about the manual-flight program, and got it patched through to my console.

I was thinking about Shanto. A good friend on Spoke, he'd joked me out of my shyness and isolation. He listened when I talked about my family and coached me for my exams. Without him, I would have washed out — and been back on Earth with my family, and Greenspit.

Now there were just the sparks of his intelligence in my memory. Now I had to be worthy of his trust. A hijacker he might have been, but I had to know his reasons. And that meant thinking of something ... suitably Jovian.

I accessed basic data on my console. Jove (or Jupiter) was the supreme god of the ancient Greeks. Even *I* knew that. I remembered Shanto talking about the gods, saying that human psychology wanted them as much now as then. So I accessed further and up came the place where the gods were supposed to live. A mountain in Greece.

'Mount Olympus?' I said hopefully.

No response, but an odd sense that the silence around me was listening.

Alright. Their mountain home would be too easy and Shanto never made things easy. So I accessed all the gods and spoke both the Roman and Greek versions of their names: Ares/Mars, Zeus/Jupiter, Athena/Minerva, Venus/Aphrodite ... I rattled them off, even all the moons of Jupiter, then the solar system.

Nothing. I could almost hear Shanto laughing. He would never make it that easy.

Something suitably Jovian ... Shanto's long finger circling ... like an orbit? The staged gesture could mean anything. Linked to Jupiter but complex. Even the made-up name of the first far-sighted Stone Age human who saw this giant star.

The first man?

Jupiter had always been visible in our heavens, but one man had looked at Jupiter through a hand-made telescope and suffered for it. But I could still hear Shanto's laughter as I spoke it aloud.

'Galileo?'

No response. Well, maybe that was too simple. Then suddenly, locked into the chess-game that was Shanto's mind, it was as if something came online in my brain. I said the name again and nothing happened. I tried endless variations, nicknames, dialects, whatever. Perhaps the answer was obvious; Shanto was devious enough for that. Clever enough to push the answer into my face. I hit the intercom and Redgrove's face came on-screen. He'd done a unit in ancient astronomy.

'Yes, Commander?' The same smooth formal voice, aware that everyone was listening.

'I'm doing a report on our mission.' I paused. 'Thought I'd mention the discoverer Galileo.'

'He'd love that, Commander. Pity he died about five hundred years ago.'

'I need to check his first name.'

'Galileo *was* his first name, Commander. Would you like his surname?'

Redgrove was scoring but I had to take it. 'Yes, Redgrove, I would.'

'*Galilei*, Commander.'

'Thank you, Redgrove.'

I shut the intercom. Simple and complex was always Shanto's style. Like someone so famous that nobody thought past his first name. Somebody who was indeed 'suitably Jovian'. It might be another Shanto trick, but I cleared my throat and spoke aloud, very self-conciously, 'Galileo Galilei?'

'Buon giorno, giovane.'

'Giovane?' I learned later that meant 'kid, young person, someone not mature'. The hologram-points in the corner shimmered into life again.

Now an old man was standing in the far corner of my cabin. His hologram-background extended to a stool, a shelf piled with thick leather-bound books and rolls of yellow parchment, and a second shelf cluttered with metal and glass objects. He was dressed in a worn black-cloth robe, a high-necked yellow linen shirt visible over the collar. He had a craggy and big-nosed face, and his brownish-red hair was streaked with grey. Alert brown eyes sparkled with curiosity.

'Ah, I don't speak Italian.'

'Then I shall speak English,' he replied. 'Courtesy of Signore Shanto Santana, of course.'

In fact, all of him was courtesy of Shanto. In between bionic reactions Shanto made hologram-creations, the latest fad on Earth and Spoke, three-dimensional historical figures programmed to hold actual conversations. They were smart enough to sort out the key words in questions, and respond to body-language and facial expressions. They were almost as real as the originals.

On Spoke, Shanto had created Joan of Arc, John Lennon, Joseph Stalin, Adolph Hitler, Elvis Presley, and all the American presidents you could think of. And within the limits of response, he could talk to them as real people. They were Shanto's own special touch of genius.

Spoke — a lifetime ago now.

Galileo! I pulled my thoughts back to the old man standing gravely waiting for my response. He had a superior bearing to him, as though it was a privilege for me to be in the same room as him. He was *real*!

'You are Galileo Galilei?'

'Sired Galilei,' he corrected heavily. We were not on first-name terms. 'I am instructed to introduce myself as the holographic representation of the ship's control system.' He paused. 'I am also instructed to inform you that I cannot divulge direct information without Signore Shanto's permission.'

'Shanto is dead.'

Galileo shrugged. 'That is regrettable. But it is not a factor allowing for a program clearance.'

'So you can't tell me anything?' I yelled.

'If you choose to so interpret it,' replied the Galileo-hologram, managing to imply that it was my intellectual limitations that were the problem. I abruptly downlined him.

Wonderful! My only voice-link to the ship's systems was a Renaissance astronomer who would tell me nothing.

I thought hard for a few minutes. The three-dimensional hologram of Galileo seemed so real that my white-walled unit seemed empty without him. My head hurt. I was in command but I knew nothing, and Jupiter and the black solid nothing of outer space was outside.

There was no point in summoning Galileo back. Shanto would have programmed the pontificating old windbag too well. And I was the commander, and I needed to get back to the flight-deck. I was about to contact Elissa via the intercom when some instinct stopped me, and I adjusted the console to see what she was doing.

It was nothing she had told me about; she'd even screened it from my console readouts.

I watched for a few moments. She was using the hull visual systems with skill and method, quartering each square centimetre of the hull. At one point the scanners uptilted a little and I glimpsed Reliant's spacesuit-figure in the background. She was looking for something around the spacesuit — maybe trapped by the inert gravity — and doing it when she thought I was occupied elsewhere. That was interesting.

I offscreened, counted to ten, then opened the intercom. 'Status, Elissa?'

There was a pause, just long enough to offline the scanners, then she appeared onscreen. 'Status normal, signals from the probe are good, nothing to report.'

'Log that. I'm coming back.'

I checked the cabin and re-coded the lock. Nobody was getting in here except me. And Elissa could keep her little secret — until I found out what it was. It was lucky I had decided not to trust anyone.

On the control deck, Elissa was watching a pitted grey surface on the after-scanners. Callisto. 'Quite a strong gravitational field,' she said. 'Just the tips of our probe's antennae are showing. Chances of a meteor-strike are zero.'

I upscreened the control readouts; there was nothing there about the hull scanners. Elissa looked at me curiously and I changed the subject — clumsily.

'Got a family telecast when I was going under cryo. They're quarantined.'

Nine months ago I'd got that telecast. And for the first time I admitted to myself that they were all dead. Quarantine hadn't stopped Greenspit anywhere.

'All telecast signals ceased in my Earth-quadrant a month before our take-off,' she said quietly, even calmly, but her hands knotted tightly together. 'I … I heard a rumour just before take-off that a new plague was starting. Something called Blackroot.'

Another!

Elissa unclasped her hands. 'I heard another rumour, just a whisper, before I went under cryo. There was a case of Greenspit reported in Spoke.'

'How the hell would Greenspit get into Spoke?'

'We know nothing about these viral plagues — what causes them, how they travel, even how long they've been dormant in our bodies.'

All the more reason to contact Spoke. Flying the spaceship without that instant voice-ac response was tough enough, but Shanto's dead brain also blocked our telecast channels.

As I watched that grey surface of Callisto, I remembered Ciardh's poem. *We explore other planets but let our world die.* Callisto had orbited for billions of years and knew nothing of Earth or the mountains of dead. Now Blackroot, perhaps mountains more. A hand touched mine.

'I'm sorry about your family.'

There was a tear in Elissa's eye. We hadn't liked each other much on Spoke. I swear she fouled me at the netball finals. She was one of Cybele Reliant's elite. 'Amazons', Shanto called them, and because he didn't like her, neither did I. I just nodded and she took her hand away.

Redgrove's voice came suddenly on the intercom, as sarcastic as ever. It was a useful jolt to clear my head. 'Commander, since you're back on deck, can we come out of our cabins?'

'Pity it wasn't him who disappeared,' Elissa said softly. Her small smile was pure tension.

'Yes, clear cabins, report for assignments.' We were all uptight. Too much of this mission was a deadly, unknown puzzle. Then I remembered something. 'Simon, how did that scan go?'

A pause, then Simon's voice, sounding shaky. 'Doing it, Commander. I'm checking Protus —'

Elissa sat up sharply. 'Simon, you did that half an hour ago.'

His voice was confused, even sleepy, as though we'd just woken him up. 'No, I'm re-checking Protus, something I —' And his voice ended in a strange gurgling gasp.

'Simon!' There was a dry rasping sound that went right through me. 'Elissa, take control!'

I was already out of my chair, running as quickly down the passage as my boots would let me. It was a long passage and everybody had heard the intercom. Conception appeared at her door, then Redgrove, then Belinda. Simon's door was ahead now, still closed. I pressed the button to release the door — nothing happened.

'Elissa!'— shouting at the door intercom unit —'Open!'

Her voice was taut, close to panic. 'Nothing. Systems over-ride!'

Now the *manual* systems were not working? 'Must be a glitch. Locate it!' I slammed the button this time. Nothing.

Belinda, Redgrove and Conception crowded behind me, their boots clanging. Then through the door came a thin electronic whining, and Elissa, the panic real in her voice, said, 'The ventilation system's working. That's an override too!'

I felt as if the air around me was thick and choking. I slammed the button hard and this time we heard the offlining click. The ventilation whine stopped and the door slid open. Redgrove was beside me, his voice sharp with horror, all the cynicism gone.

'Hell —'

Nothing from Conception and Belinda. We were all looking at the impossible thing in front of us. Elissa's voice came through, sharp with horror, forgetting my rank.

'Declan, no life-readings in the cabin.'

'No,' I heard myself answer back, my words sounding flat. 'You won't get any.'

Ahead of me, in the cabin, floated a pale, four-tentacled something. A glove bobbed in the weightless gravity, another beside it, and near it stood Simon's tracksuit. 'Stood', although the ends of his trousers were clear of his boots. In each boot was a sock.

But in tracksuit, gloves and boots there was no trace of Simon. Even more horrible, above the zipped neckline of the tracksuit floated a pair of metal-rimmed spectacles, as though supported by an invisible head.

Simon's body had vanished. Just in that first moment I thought I glimpsed a speckle of dust above the collar, like a ghastly disintegrated impression of a human face. Then it faded to nothing.

Simon was gone — like Shanto.

FIVE

> *So I know more about you now, onscreen-Declan. Ciardh, Mum and Dad, you know they are dead. It's in the way you spoke. And Simon's gone but he was colourless, precise. Shanto, check on him, he was too vibrant and smart just to die.*
>   *'Why would I be checking the hull?' whispered Elissa beside me.*
>   *Why? I can think of a reason, so can onscreen-Declan. But I won't tell her because there are secrets now between us. Just as he has secrets with his Elissa. But he knows where those secrets will lead and I'm thinking I should have a hand-laser.*

I sent Conception up to the controls, and got Elissa to come down with a hand-scanner. She went over the cabin, and showed me the readouts in a small screen set in the handle.

'Some minor chemical readouts. Salts mainly.'

'The ventilation system operated,' said Belinda from the door. 'Would that have —'

'Micro-filtered?' said Elissa. 'A human body breaking down sufficiently to pass through that?' She shrugged, not from lack of interest but from the same disquiet that gripped us all. 'Broken down into its component molecules?'

'He couldn't just vanish!' shot back Belinda. 'Nothing could cause that!'

'A latent after-effect of cryo-sleep,' muttered Redgrove. 'Relaxing us too much?'

'Nice joke, Redgrove, in the usual good taste,' I replied. 'You and Belinda get to after-control, and see if you can isolate that override.'

He didn't want to go and neither did Belinda. But they clopped off down the passage. I offlined the intercom, not wanting Conception to hear this.

'Elissa, most improbable scenario. Alien of some type, virus or —'

'Fossil traces of a few bacilli on Mars,' she said. 'Maybe something on Jupiter's moons, but nothing strong enough to come into *Copernicus*. We'd all be infected.'

'So?' I pointed.at Simon's empty suit which still hung in the air.

Elissa just set her lips and held up her hand-scanner. 'This is not a crystal ball.'

She was cool. I had to admire that. We unzipped the suit, checked the boots and socks. Nothing. What were Simon's last words? 'Protus —'

'He said he was scanning the systems, Commander. I did too, before coming down here. Normal, nothing irregular.'

And there was no reason why the cabin door would not open, or why the air-filter activated. I was about to bring the intercom online when Elissa stopped me. She glanced around as she spoke, her voice low.

'There's something else. Just before Simon's life-readouts stopped registering, there was a ... a surge of some kind in the cabin.' She paused, frowning, trying to find the right words. 'Like ... like an extra reading of warmth and substance. As though something was in the room with him.'

There was a new note in her voice, of caution, even fear? Well, I was feeling that myself. We stepped back into the corridor. Behind us, Simon's floating spectacles glinted with a mocking intelligence. I shut the door.

'If there was a "presence" in the cabin, it's not there now. He was talking about Protus —'

'Protus is fine.'

'We should check.'

'We already have.'

Back on the flight-deck, Conception was at the controls and Callisto was still on the after-scanners. Now the shadow of another moon passed over it — Ganymede.

'Six hours before the next course-change,' she said.

I nodded and turned to Elissa. She knew what I was going to say and glared at me like a mother lion defending her cub.

'Visual check on Protus, Elissa. It should be used to the light by now. Routine, Elissa.'

I said that lightly and she took her cue. Neither of us wanted Conception starting rumours; she was just too pally with Redgrove. So she nodded and we even checked the bridge readouts before going down just to keep things looking normal. Even though nothing was normal.

It was time to see if something else was in the tank with Protus.

* * *

Protus Intacta. Okay, you all know about Protus, but even the details of how Protus came about are vital in this report.

Last century the first deep-sea exploration craft were called bathyspheres; they were round tubs of steel, steel being the only metal that could withstand the enormous pressures at those depths. In about 1930 a Doctor William Beebe went two kilometres down, deeper than life was thought to exist. But he saw fish, unknown species, living where the pressure was about a tonne per square metre. In the 1990s the probes went as deep as it got and there was still life: species whose bodies were adapted to cope with incredible pressures. This led to answers when the exploration of Jupiter was planned.

Jupiter has a gravity equal to the planet's mass: a hundred times greater than any Earth-ocean. Our new probes had super-tough alloys, stressed to resist the most intense pressure. Even so, they were atomised out of existence by Jupiter's gravity. So something new had to be designed. And the something new was Protus.

It was Shanto's idea. Clone something from the gene-cell of a deep-sea species and bio-restructure it into something much bigger, something with the body-stress necessary to withstand Jupiter's pressures.

Idea? No, genius. Because where a probe could not go a life-form could — to access the most incredible stock of scientific knowledge ever gained: how the universe was put together, how planets came into being.

Protus was designed and 'created' in the Spoke labs. Shanto worked alone at first, then with Elissa and some others. There had been pressure on Shanto to include them, mostly from the stroppy bunch around Reliant. And maybe no one liked the idea of Shanto controlling too much. They were scared of his genius.

We were below-decks and in front of the tank. The area was fully lit now and the murky red fluid had cleared to a rich ruby colour. And there swam Protus. State-of-the-art, maybe, but also just about the ugliest thing you could imagine.

It was six metres in length, with a massive rounded body and rows of sensor-teeth that set an undershot jaw in a permanent droopy snarl. Running along each side were lateral rows of photophore cells; each emitted a pale light, like the portholes of an ocean liner. One pair of long antennae quivered at the anal fin, the other at the lower jaws. They glowed like headlamps, their natural light generated by Protus.

Its big, blinking saucer eyes could record data, transmit it to the 'brain', and boost it to the Callisto relay and then Earth. Those eyes were like two-way cameras, recording Jupiter's chemical make-up as Protus swam in the oceans and even touched the rocky core of the planet. All the secrets of the planet would be ours.

'Large as life and twice as ugly,' I muttered.

Elissa did not reply. She had no sense of humour where Protus was concerned. This nightmare composition of animal life was moving now, flapping its fins in a demonstration of awesome contained power. Did those bulging eyeballs swivel in our direction?

'How come it's moving?' I asked. 'We haven't activated the brain stimulus yet.'

'Weren't you fully briefed, Commander? Protus needs

enough independent movement capacity to establish itself in Jupiter's oceans.' She paused, raising her eyebrows. 'Well, do you see anything in the tank? Even one bug-eyed alien?'

'Careful, Elissa, you nearly made a joke about Protus.' Our boots clanged on the floor as we went back to the ladder. Then I remembered. 'Cryo tank?'

'Yes. Five degrees below zero, so wrap up warmly if you're going for a swim, Commander.' She paused on the first step of the ladder, her face expressionless. 'Oh dear, I nearly made another joke.'

There was another movement from the tank as Elissa led the way up up the ladder, as though Protus was watching us. We resealed the hatch and the full bizarre horror of our situation came back. We had been all over the ship and there was no sign of Simon, or his killer. And as I thought that, I couldn't help thinking something else.

Who would be next?

That thought came back even more strongly on the flight-deck. Scanning and search had revealed nothing. Who would be the next to just disappear?

'Europa!' That was Belinda, in the third control chair.

Below and thousands of kilometres closer to Jupiter's own orbit was another moon. It was perfectly round, a light blue colour with criss-crossing dark lines.

'Readouts confirm it's only ten per cent ice,' she said. This was her job and she was fascinated, intent. 'Albedo .70, smoothest ice surface in the solar system. We think there's a water ocean underneath.'

'Frozen solid?' asked Redgrove.

Belinda shook her head. 'No. Ganymede pulls it slightly off orbit every second turn, and heats it up enough to maintain a liquid ocean.'

'So there could be life — real life?' asked Conception.

'Maybe. Just like Earth's first oceans.'

We were really too young for a mission like this, and we had more problems than we could handle. But we were explorers and that was Europa moon below. For long minutes the magic held us close, fascinated us and touched our hearts with awe. For long minutes we were just big kids.

'That bloody spacesuit!' Conception's sharp voice pierced the silence. One of the monitor screens had Commander Reliant's spacesuit in visual, a horrible reminder of how she had died. That broke the spell.

'We could disconnect the boot-controls, but inert gravity would still keep it by the ship.' I was the commander. I had to keep them thinking. 'I want a manual backup in rear control. All three of you, keep in sight of each other. Elissa will patch it through.'

They left and I sat there thinking. I had strung Shanto's disc around my neck. I wanted nobody seeing that. Something came into my mind. I had to play this cool, not let Elissa suspect anything.

I sighed. A long and weary sigh. 'Maybe I should check cabin cryo-readouts. Might be a clue there. Will you be alright alone?'

She nodded. 'I'll be fine. I don't vanish easily.'

Was there a note of relief in her voice? Her fingers moved slightly, as though itching to be back at her hull-scanning. She even managed a smile.

I went back to my cabin. It didn't matter if Elissa found

what she was scanning for; she couldn't get to it without my help.

Back in the cabin I checked. Yes, she was scanning the hull, and she also had the other three on visual in the rear. She was taking no chances of being discovered. I nearly smiled. At least she couldn't ask Galileo.

I thought about that irritating old codger. And suddenly I glanced over to the hologram-receiving points in the corner and remembered his pompous voice resounding through the cabin. How had he phrased it? *Could not divulge direct information.*

Direct? Shanto had programmed a thinking hologram for his console, but, being Shanto, had he hidden a teasing subtext even into this. No direct answers. *Think all ways, Declan. Nothing is obvious!* Perhaps his Galileo-hologram could *hint* at answers. This meant that to get anywhere I had to out-think Shanto *and* Galileo. Another check showed Elissa still at her hull-scanning, the others at their programming.

'Galileo Galilei.'

The hologram-receiving points shimmered into sparkling life. The old boy appeared, blinking a little irately as though annoyed at the disturbance. He did not speak but curled his lip and waited.

I swallowed hard and made myself smile. 'A great honour to meet you, Signor Galilei,' I said. 'Please forgive my earlier discourtesy in offlining you so abruptly.'

'The young are often rash,' he replied loftily. 'And seldom good-mannered.' But he did give a gratified smile. Yes, as conceited as Shanto could program him.

'I should have been more courteous to such a great scholar,' I replied, longing to kick his hologram-butt.

'So my name is not unknown to you?' He smiled smugly.

'Jupiter is ahead of us,' I said. 'We are passing the moons you discovered.'

Yes, Shanto had excelled himself with this creation. There was something very human in Galileo's reaction. There was a more genuine smile and proud joy in the brown eyes, and his manner was less annoying, even wistful. 'I have seen them only as specks of light,' he said, 'my telescope just the length of my arm. But in my hands, it became an eye on the cosmos.'

And using that telescope brought you a lot of real trouble from the Holy Catholic Church, I thought. And I still felt the wonder of talking to Galileo. There was something even comic and appealing in the way he drew himself up to his full height and continued talking — well, declaiming really.

'I was the greatest astronomer of my age. I corresponded with princes, popes and kings. I was — am — a master mathematician and skilled in mechanics. I measured the mountains of the moon. I designed an oil lamp and invented the thermometer.' Galileo stroked his beard in that self-important way. A gold chain gleamed around his collar. 'I defined the shape of Purgatory, the antechamber of Hell, from the writings of Dante —'

He went on talking and I thought hard. Shanto did nothing without a reason; he didn't create Galileo just for the historical associations. Three crew-members gone, the mission in real danger. How could I find out what I needed to know — indirectly? Galileo was still going on about the clever way he measured Purgatory.

'— a cone, consisting of a sector one-twelfth the size of the earth. Purgatory is the home of Lucifer, Prince of Darkness, who stands locked in ice, his navel forming the exact centre of the Earth —'

'Signore Galilei,' I interrupted gently, 'you cannot directly divulge information, but what about an *indirect* answer?'

He looked at me, puzzled. Okay, here goes, I thought. 'From what you know of ship-systems and crew-movement, will I find Shanto's personal disc in or around Commander Reliant's spacesuit?'

Galileo's craggy face had set in shrewd lines. Then he shrugged and his mouth curved in a mocking smile. 'Young man ...' the words uttered in such a condescending way that my heart sank, 'it would be advisable to gain intelligence before attempting to match wits with me. I have given you my answer.'

'You could at least try, if you're that bloody clever.'

'I am clever.' He hooked one long brown finger into his gold chain and almost smirked. 'You, on the other hand, are not. Otherwise you would not seek to beguile me with such a clumsy subterfuge.'

Unreal. I was having an argument with a smart-arse hologram. 'I just want to know!'

'Then open your eyes and use your brain, assuming you have one.' He tugged on his gold chain and smiled. 'Knowledge is power, young man. Excuse me now, I shall downline.'

I stood up. 'Signore Galilei, you downline when I say so —'

A shimmer and he was gone, but not without an amused look and a little bow. I nearly raised him again, then hesitated. Open my eyes and use my brain? And that mocking smile like Shanto's, hooking his finger in the gold chain.

My too-sensible Declan, think laterally, he would say, hooking a finger into the cord of his personal disc in exactly the same way. And then it hit me, slammed me like Elissa knocking me off-court in the Spoke finals.

Open your eyes, think laterally!

Galileo, Shanto's hologram, recorded and watched but could not answer directly. Open your eyes? Did a finger hooked in a cord, or in a gold chain, tell me where Reliant had put the disc, repository of all Shanto's secrets?

The simplest, safest place to keep it would be looped around her own neck.

Open your eyes, *think laterally!* Nothing is as it seems!

It was stupid not to have thought of it earlier. And Elissa had figured it out before me. That was what she was hull-scanning for — Shanto's disc.

A body vanishing was not what it seemed to be. Perhaps Reliant did not implode, which would explain why her remains were not trapped by the inert hull gravity. *What if she'd vanished like the others!* Then the disc would be in her spacesuit, or held nearby by gravity.

'Shanto, you incredibly complex piece of work.' Saying it aloud made me feel better. Yes, complex and brilliant, more layers than a cosmic onion. Even in death he was helping me, prompting his creation to solve the riddle of his own murder. And presenting new problems.

I had to go out onto the spaceship hull and check for that disc. But I had to find a way of doing it without the others knowing, especially Elissa. Maybe she was an enemy, maybe just working to her own agenda. But if I went out onto the hull, I might never find out.

I might never come back.

SIX

> *Onscreen-Declan leans back in the chair a moment. He wants to shut his eyes but doesn't. Elissa and I are transfixed, finding out about ourselves. He doubts himself, trying to find his way through a complex puzzle. He is me, but would I do those things? I just don't know.*
>
> *I can't remember. Nor can Elissa, but will she remember first? She is the opponent — not the enemy, I won't use that word yet — our body-language says so. She sits taut, away from me, lets onscreen-Declan unfold the horror in his croaking voice. As he gulps more of those capsules, it hits me. 'He's afraid of vanishing — like the others!'*

Bluish-grey Europa, its surface like fine cracks in porcelain, was passing below when I called everyone back to the flight deck.

Ahead of and overlapping the moon, Jupiter's orbit brought the famed Red Spot into view again. Stormy, blood-shot and twice as big as Earth, nobody knew what it was — yet. Protus would tell us for sure — *if* we managed to launch Protus.

I was thinking about that when everyone assembled. I told them what I wanted and, naturally, Redgrove reacted first.

'Confining everyone to quarters!' he yelled. 'That's a state of arrest!'

He was right, of course, so I had to lie, my earnest words sounding like the truth. I explained that I wanted them to stay in the cabins in pairs so that nobody would be alone, and if whatever happened to Simon happened again we would get some clues.

Copernicus was built for a bigger crew and each cabin had a second let-down bunk. None of the crew were happy. Nobody likes being reminded that they might suddenly disappear. Belinda even pointed out that we were still not certain that Simon was dead — even though there was nowhere he could be hiding.

'So we don't leave our cabins without permission?' asked Conception, uptight and frowning as always.

'No, Conception.' A rest period was scheduled, even though nobody needed it yet. Elissa and Redgrove would be in one cabin, Belinda and Conception in another. Elissa was the last to go, not without a doubting look at me and a last word at the door.

'You'll bring me out for the turn?'

'Of course, Elissa.'

The turn. The reason why I had to act now. *Copernicus*, still flying on its original program, must turn to get closer to Jupiter-orbit for the launch of Protus. And when *Copernicus* made that turn, anything held in the hull's inert gravity would be left behind. She would know that.

So I set the controls and patched a relay through to a

wrist-console. We normally used the wrist-consoles only in emergencies, but this was one. I could talk to the others on audio and fool them into thinking I was still inside the spaceship. I didn't want any conversation, but Redgrove — bless him — solved that. He was no sooner in his cabin than he called on the intercom.

'Commander, what about calls of nature?'

'Find something in the cabin. I'm sure Elissa's seen it all before. No other unnecessary remarks, please.'

There was a low chuckle from Elissa and I cut the intercom. I scanned quickly to ensure that they were all settled then took off my boots and kicked silently to my cabin. Once in my spacesuit I set the mini-console in my helmet and strapped a readout-unit to my wrist. I floated myself down to the lower deck, through the storage-units and to the starboard outer airlock.

I went through the inner airlock and sealed it shut behind me. The outer lock had an oval porthole, framing the deep blackness of outer space. Going out alone was extremely risky, but I had too many questions and no answers. I pressed the manual release and the outer airlock opened.

This was even more risky. Everyone thought their commander was sitting, brooding and insecure, on the flight-deck. The airlock slid open and I spoke into the intercom. 'Status normal, on course.'

I made it terse and snappy, not inviting reply. Auto transmission would offend them even more, their commander not showing his face on visual now.

I'd been out the airlock dozens of times before, from Spoke basic-training to moon flights. But it was always with the reassuring bulk of something close and comrades ready. Even so, the transition from spaceship to deep space was always sudden.

Seeing deep space through the observation port is one thing, but having overwhelming blackness engulf you like a vast alien ocean is another. But *Copernicus* was on the turn, I was on the flank of the giant beast, and I had little time.

I walked out across the hull. Behind me were the moons we had passed, Callisto a large grey coin in the background. Around me spread the infinite blackness of space, set with brilliant stars — layer upon layer of stars like myriad shoals of solar fireflies — and the distant blue-white streak of a comet. Earth itself was a mere point of light among billions. The nearest was Saturn, glowing blue-green even at that distance. I was human, insignificant and tiny.

I began to walk over the hull. The magnetic-soled boots held me easily as I set off towards the big tail-fin. It was a long walk, and the only sound was my heavy breathing in the suit. I was able to see up to the end of that silver-plate highway, to where the spacesuit-figure stood. As I trudged towards it, the blackness and silver fire-shoals around me, a blazing orange–red edge tipped over the raised centre backbone of the hull — the awesome blazing majesty of Jupiter.

There was no time to stand and watch. But for a moment nothing could move me. I stared at the huge flaring mass of the planet: a monster orb, banded white, orange, brown-red, and inset with that huge Red Spot, like a cyclops' glaring eye.

Clouds of ammonia crystal covered the surface and below those were red clouds of another chemical. Below that, the planet-rotation produced an energy-field as strong as the sun. How Jupiter even stayed together was a mystery. All that bursting energy radiated towards us, mocking us and our puny Earth-made craft edging so warily towards it.

It was hypnotic and chilling, like a blazing hell, gigantic and untamed. But inside our insignificant Earth-craft was a specially created organism that would penetrate the planet's secrets — challenge that majesty.

I turned and began walking down the hull to where the spacesuit was, outlined black against the flaring red. It waited. Was it only my imagination that made me think the helmet-head inclined very slightly in my direction? Both Reliant's suit and mine were now outlined in the flashing red Jupiter-light, and a curious unease crawled over my skin. I spoke tersely into my helmet-link to the wrist-console.

'Status normal.'

Again there was a pointed silence. Not that I cared. Now I was close to the spacesuit; the helmet-space uncovered by the visor looked back like a huge black eye. The helmet flashed redly but there was nothing inside that visor-space. Not even the tiny suggestion of a dust-face that I saw when Simon vanished.

I shuffled closer. It took all my resolve to reach forward with one gloved hand, push it into the oval darkness as though down an endless black throat. I clutched around and feel something tangle in my fingers.

Yes! Inside, bobbing like Simon's spectacles, were Shanto's disc and cord.

Something flashed. The suit readouts activated! I snatched my hand out as the helmet-visor snapped shut. Just as horribly, the spacesuit figure put up a hand and tore the lead off my oxygen-pack. I gulped, the air instantly gone. As I stepped back, disc-cord in one hand, the thing followed, now grabbing for my utility-pack.

Pure instinct had made me take the step back, and now training took over as I thumbed the backup pack — just thirty minutes of air. I took another backward step as that gloved hand lunged again at my suit-control. If it got that, I'd lose all life-support systems. Think, think. *An empty spacesuit was coming to life!*

Not just spacesuits, I told myself, more like hollow androids. They were lined with micro-circuits, even the gloves, making them into live empty hands. And whoever controlled those hands was intent on murder.

I yelled into my helmet but nothing happened. I yelled again. No answer. The same override that locked Simon's door was suddenly back in force. I backed away again as the spacesuit-thing stepped towards me, Jupiter-light a red glaring eye in its visor.

I kept backing away, my breathing loud in my helmet. Short breaths to save the air. This thing was keeping me from the airlock and I had to think — *think*. It only had to grab me and hold me until my air was used up. Jupiter looked on as Reliant's suit forced me back again, against the tail-fin.

Think! I couldn't move quickly in a spacesuit — but I had to. Think. Each wrist had a small magnetic clasp like the boot-sole, a backup in case the boots failed. I looped the cord over my wrist, thumbed each magnetic clasp in turn, then pointed my arms at the hull. The magnetic clasps pulled me down. I tore up my boots so that only the circuits in the tip held. Both hands were on the hull, as though I had fallen forward.

Squinting up through my visor, I could see the spacesuit-figure marching towards me. Whoever controlled it would be unsure, maybe think my backup tank had failed. Control-lights still winked on those marching boots. Their manual controls still functioned — that was good. So I lay still, my breath hard, as the thing loomed over me. That blank red eye looked down. I tore my wrists free, grabbed the booted ankles and flicked the controls to zero.

The thing was bending over, the gloved hands nearly at my backup-pack. Wrenching my own hands free, I grabbed those horrible empty wrists and pulled myself up. My own visor was against the reflected red eye as I released the wrist and ripped the oxygen line away. The thing was snatched suddenly up.

Only the full power of my boots on the hull stopped me from following it. An empty suit does not need oxygen, but the air lost from that ruptured line was like a miniature jet-stream. Up it went, out of the hull's inert gravity, to be grabbed by the awesome power of Jupiter's orbit. That same giant unseen hand closed around me and I thumbed the boot circuits to full power, then looked up.

Above, a tiny glass-faced spacesuit doll twisted and turned, jerked as though on the end of an invisible line. It was only a few hundred metres away but hopelessly lost, unable to return. It would orbit Jupiter for thousands of years until drawn close enough to be atomised by the planet's gravity.

My throat was dry and sweat misted my visor. I gulped air, shaking. My readout said eighteen minutes of oxygen left, but it felt like I'd been battling the spacesuit-thing for an hour. There was no time to think about that. I let the huge dazzle of Jupiter drop behind me as I clumped back down the side of the hull to the airlock.

Fifteen minutes of oxygen left. Twelve minutes. As I reached the outer lock, it suddenly slid shut. The operational lights winked off. I was locked out.

No manual systems, no voice-ac. And nobody to come to my help because I'd taken good care to be isolated on the flight-deck. Their power-tripping commander was turning the spaceship himself, so there would be nobody looking out for me. Turning the spaceship! And even as I thought this, side-panels slid open under the tail-fins and the turning boosters came out. *Copernicus* was making ready for its turn, *but early*!

Of course. Whoever controlled the ship intended just that, hoping that the movement would throw me off, send me spinning towards Jupiter like that spacesuit-thing. And even if I hung on somehow, soon — nine minutes of air left — I'd be finished anyway. And the only way to access the ship's data-banks for help was through the mouth of a long-dead Italian astronomer.

'Galileo Galilei?'

There was no way his hologram-image could project, but his voice boomed eerily in the helmet ear-circuits. 'As a fellow celestial voyager, you may now call me by my first name. I will online to Galileo.'

'Ah yeah, thanks — honoured.' I tried to sound grateful but every breath brought death closer. 'I'm outside, entry systems sealed. Any way back in? Quick!'

'Young man!' My heart sank at those pontificating words. I could almost see them being framed on his bearded lips. 'Signore Leonardo da Vinci designed a primitive flying machine. That is my sole link to your own craft and it did not work. You might as well compare a hole in the ground to a modern flush latrine. Goodbye.'

If loud abusive language about obnoxious holograms could have got me inside, then the next ten seconds would have done it. He at least gave me a hint last time! I had the disc but I was finished because Shanto's creation was too damn close to the original. Spouting crap about flush toilets! Then Shanto's words came to me: *You never think laterally, Declan!*

Toilets! Modern version of a hole in the ground. Waste material in outer space, always a problem. So we —

Then it registered. *That's what he was talking about!*

Inert gravity again. The waste-system always flushed on a turn so the waste material would be left behind. Even the little from our sleeping bodies, built up over nine months, had to be got rid of.

That wonderful cunning old fox!

The exhaust systems were too distant for the minutes of oxygen I had left. It was too far to walk. Turning, I downlined the boot controls and pressed the little wrist air-jets — emergency use only — draining more air from my backup. I needed just a quick spurt to skim me back up the hull, keeping very close, arms and legs wide.

The tail-fin angled up now like a giant axe-blade. *Copernicus* had an anatomical design — the eject vent was just below the tail exhaust. There also, set in the gleaming lizard-skin hull, was a simple manual control set for ground-staff inspection. It was coded, but I knew the code. *A minute or less left!* A last touch on the jets, angling sideways, then I was thumbing the code — hoping like hell that the main systems did not override it. Yes, it was working! I scrambled inside, grabbing the handholds put there for maintenance. But I remembered another problem! The engine-blast when altering course would turn this vent into an oven.

Ahead, the second vent-lock opened, and a blast of unmentionable body waste from the months of cryo-sleep streamed around me like a flood. I grabbed the edges of the second hatch as it began to close, thrusting my helmeted head inside. The hatch was strong. I could almost hear the helmet cracking as I pushed my shoulders through. The suit was slimy with brown waste as I wriggled into the second airlock, forcing myself through.

I rolled into the main processing chamber and flipped open my visor. The air stank in here, but at least it was air. Gagging, I staggered forward, because in moments the sun-hot energy of the engines would sear through this place. Around me there was a humming and vibrating movement as though *Copernicus* had taken a deep breath.

Moments!

I somehow tottered over the rounded chamber-floor, opened the next hatch, and kicked it shut behind me. *The heat would still cook me!* I was at the last hatch and *Copernicus* vibrated again. Slamming my visor back down, I scrambled through and clanged the hatch shut. In a nano-second the incandescent heat would have vaporised me.

I was safe. Only the super-insulation of my suit had saved me and it was burned black. Separated by a half-metre of alloy was the white-hot sun-glare of killing radiance, flaring just that moment to set *Copernicus* on the new course.

I stank, I was scorched and I ached all over. The tears rolled down my dirty cheeks. There was no time to relax, though. I checked the systems, and they were back to normal. Of course, my would-be killer thought I was gone. There was a monitor here, and it was unusual for Belinda not to be watching her precious engines. I had a lot to do, and quickly. There was one thing to say, though, clearly and distinctly in the silence.

'Thank you, Galileo.'

There was no answer, of course, but I could just feel the smugness. Well, this time he was entitled. I pulled off my spacesuit and left it floating there. I went into the little shower-unit the engine staff used, tracksuit and all. The tracksuit was synthetic and would dry quickly enough. Being wet reminded me I was still alive.

I climbed the ladder to the lower deck. As I walked past the tank where Protus floated, it goggled at me incuriously, unaware of all that had happened. Soon, I thought, we could put the blasted fish where it belonged. Shanto's disc was now around my neck, tucked well inside my collar.

I cut the boots at the top and went weightless, breast-stroking down the corridor so the others wouldn't hear my boots. My wrist-console had been smashed on the way back in — maybe they'd been trying to call. The cabin readouts showed everyone still inside their units.

I slipped into the control chair. Jupiter was still ahead, at a slightly different angle. We were set now for that final pass, skirting the close gravity to release Protus. Elissa's voice came loudly on the intercom, as if she'd been shouting for some time.

'Declan, for the last time! Do you copy?'

'Wait a minute. Turn completed, status normal.'

'So why are we being kept in our cabins?' Redgrove sounded angry. A little too angry? 'What's going on?'

'I'm power-mad, now shut up,' I snapped.

They were well-trained and would stay put — for now. Maybe long enough for me to get some answers. I had the disc and there was an H-scanner in the control locker. Shanto's personal data would be coded tightly, but the updates from Spoke, transmitted in flight, would be there. And they might give a clue as to who the killers were.

Killers — plural.

Because whoever planned my murder must have done it from one of the cabins. There was nobody else, because repeated scans had shown we were alone, except for Protus. And two in a cabin meant that two people were involved. Redgrove and Elissa or Belinda and Conception.

And that made things worse. I could believe Redgrove, but not Elissa — even though she did have secrets. Conception maybe, but not Belinda. And not really Conception, unless Redgrove was pulling her strings. Or maybe one person had drugged their partner somehow, just long enough to send me into orbit. But even Redgrove needed more motive than dislike. No, there was something deeper here, something so deep that I still couldn't even glimpse it. But I knew one thing.

Somebody wanted me out of the way, and that somebody would try again.

SEVEN

> My onscreen-Declan leans back. There are beads of sweat on his forehead and he wipes them off. I recognise the handkerchief, a big bandana-type, a goodbye present from Ciardh.
> 'This is not real,' says Elissa beside me.
> It is real, Elissa. He went out of the spaceship and returned. I can't imagine myself having the desperate courage for that. Maybe I would have, but it's all still a total blank. And like you, onscreen-Declan, I cannot see any purpose to this. And neither can Elissa.
> Assuming that her mind is also a total blank.

I explained to the others that they should stay in their cabins a little longer, keeping each other company, the ship's systems open so they could check course. Anyway, nothing important would happen for some time yet.

And we'll be out for that, Declan?' snapped Elissa.

Long before then, I assured her, we would have a full briefing. They accepted this, a little too easily perhaps. And I caught a mutter from Redgrove about how if the guy *was* power-mad then he was better left on his own. Redgrove always did have great team spirit.

I was still not hungry or thirsty. After cryo, the body held nutrient fluids like a sponge. I offlined, thinking for a moment. Yes, it was a little easy but I couldn't worry about that now. I needed any answers I could find on Shanto's disc. First I had something else to do.

'Galileo?'

'Greetings, Declan. Or is "Commander" more proper?'

'Declan's fine.'

The flight-deck had a hologram-receiving point too. And although he was only a hologram, there was a curious pleasure in hearing that solemn voice use my first name. He was seated on his stool and balancing a pair of tiny glass scales — maybe something of his own design — and he looked like a child with a new toy.

'Thank you for saving my life,' I said, and I meant it. By now I'd have been somewhere in Jupiter-orbit, or grilled to a tiny black crisp.

His nose was almost touching the scales but up went a bristly eyebrow. '*Did* I help you?' his words sounding a little too gratified to fool me.

'You know you did, despite your programming. Can you tell me what's making our crew vanish?'

'No, Declan, I cannot.'

This was uttered simply, his brown eyes solemn. A blanket refusal without the slightest clue.

'Because of the programming?'

'Yes, Declan.'

Then up went both bristly eyebrows and he put down the

glass scales. He could not talk about the vanishings? *That meant that Shanto knew they would happen!* Or at least feared they would. I had outwitted Galileo and the lines on his face deepened to a scowl.

'Sorry, Signore,' I said, as humbly as I could.

'Never apologise for being clever!' he snapped.

Well, the Inquisition had made *him* apologise for being clever. For being a scientific genius at a time when men of science were burned at the stake. Then his scowl suddenly cleared and he smiled, and, with a graceful movement of his hand, downlined.

I opened the intercom. 'Status normal. Room service anyone?'

There was no answer but I'll bet a finger or two went up. It was time to look at Shanto's disc.

Shanto's disc was the latest V-R, Virtual-Recall. All his personal data was on deeper levels, but I was banking on him not having had time to code-lock the Spoke transmissions. Reliant knew it was important too, as she'd taken it onto the hull with her.

The V-R scanner was like a huge pair of goggles with a single oblong lens. I slipped in the disc and touched the controls. I hadn't used this model before and the sudden multicoloured lines made me blink. They snapped into an image and I was *there*, in a room with two people. A man and a woman.

The woman was in her twenties, with a strong face and round 'Spoke-saucer' hairstyle, and dressed in a patched and faded utility-suit of maroon with grey piping. She had two gold command stars, meaning she held a position of high authority. The man was younger, head shaven, and with a thin humorous face. His tracksuit was a faded blue, with one lopsided gold bar.

There were about four thousand people on Spoke and I did not know the woman. Faded and patched clothes were a sign of long residency, almost a badge of rank in themselves. I did know the man, though.

Shanto.

'Declan,' said the woman. Now I could see MORGANNA black-lettered on her tunic. 'You'll be liaising with Shanto when you see this. He'll brief you more fully. Spoke has its own agenda on this mission and I'm assured of your full loyalty.'

Speaking to me! Shanto would have patched this onto my console had he survived. I was part of his plans but, being Shanto, he hadn't bothered to inform me. There was a little smile on his face now — probably imagining my reaction. They were both seated in chairs at a light yellow table, with grey walls and a round porthole behind them, showing black space, and a bar of one of the extended 'freeways'.

'All Spokes are negotiating to become a united state. We control communications to Earth, but when they have the plagues sorted out they will want control back. We must bargain from a position of strength, and data on the outer planets is part of that. Earth has mountains of dead to clean up, and we have the perfect excuse not to allow communication. A lot may change in nine months, as Shanto knows.'

Shanto smiled at me, as lifelike as ever. Yes, a lot had changed, such as Greenspit in Spoke. Such as Shanto being dead. He was virtual-reality now, an electronic ghost. *But still so real!*

'Declan,' he said, 'Morganna has summed up very neatly.

She will patch visual updates through to my personal disc.' He paused, his face smooth. 'Be careful. Morganna will assume command here and Reliant knows nothing.'

'Assume command.' As in overthrow Spoke council? I was watching them both and, from the subtle hints of body-language, I sensed no easy relationship. Partnership came from Shanto's knowledge. Morganna leaned forward.

'Declan, updates will come through Shanto, as he said. Do not trust anyone else. The *Copernicus* mission was brought forward, even rushed. Despite screening, there may be a Stoner on board.' Her lips went rat-trap tight as she said this. 'And we think Reliant has contacted Mars-Base. The base there has practically declared independence. Shanto will need you and so do we. Protus must swim in the seas of Jupiter and give us the key to life in this universe. Goodbye.'

She reached for the cut-off but Shanto stopped her with a light, graceful touch of those long fingers.

'I'll be with you when you see this,' he said at me. 'We'll go through everything then, Declan. Life in the universe — a better way for everyone. Until then, Declan, or should I say'— he grinned — 'until now?'

It was there again, an almost unspoken resentment in Morganna's body-language. Shanto was presuming on her authority and not with her consent. And Reliant in contact with Martian rebels? *And* a Stoner on board; that made the whole mission about as safe as a fire in a fuel-tank.

The transmission had ended, but a moment later Shanto was talking from his cabin, another message patched on to the end of transmission. The little fruit-knife and a half-peeled apple floated beside him. His smile was now calculating and tight.

'Something else you should see, Declan. From another transmission. You're not going to like it.'

I put the transmission on hold and eased the scanner from my eyes for a moment. Watching hologram transmissions was sometimes a little too unreal. *Not going to like it!* But I had to see this, edited though it was, before the others wanted out of their cabins. And at the moment, Belinda's voice came online.

'Declan!' She sounded urgent. 'I must see you!'

'A few minutes, Belinda.'

I cut off. Could she be the Stoner? *If* there was one. But not even Stoners could make people vanish. I sighed and re-settled the goggles and cleared the image-hold. Shanto's face disappeared, to be replaced by blackness. Then another visual-replay came onscreen and I remembered Shanto's words again.

I was not going to like this.

This transmission was from Spoke or a relay station closer to Earth, as sharp and clear as though it had come from only a hundred metres away. The scanning camera-eye descended in swooping plunges. A dark continental shadow became a state, then a city, the city layout bridged and bordered by a sluggish river, dark with pollution. The city streets and bridges were packed with unmoving vehicles. Another swoop and I could see the vehicles parked with unmoving people inside. Closer — dead people. And I knew what I was looking at. A plague scene.

Greenspit had wiped out nearly fifty per cent of the world's population. Us, the human race. And this, something I'd not let myself think about, was the human cost. These lifeless streets crammed with vehicles, like metal lemmings, spilling onto footpaths and into malls. One big yellow bus had crashed into a shop window, the driver and passengers all seated stiffly inside.

On every flat roof surface, helicopters were parked so closely that their blades tangled; some were tilted or crashed upon each other. All were packed with those unmoving people, shadows passing over them as more helicopters arrived, big and fat-bellied, full of more passengers, descending where there was clear space. Where there was not, they settled awkwardly on the vehicles in the streets, packed with their dead and landed by remote control.

There was another plunge, taking me too close to sickening reality: not only was each vehicle packed with dead but even the roof-racks held bodies. Arms and legs were strapped tidily; I could see the upturned faces: women, men and children, all stiff and staring, smudges of green saliva on their lips.

And almost with relief, I saw a thin red spear of flame jab upwards; then others, springing sharp and vivid, flame-spears that spread so quickly that it must have been prearranged, joining into one red pool, with thick smoke blotting out the thousands and thousands of vehicles.

Shanto was showing me this to inform me and perhaps to reinforce that Earth had too many problems to be concerned with Spoke. It was transmitted without sound because this horror did not need words. This was Earth's answer to Greenspit — fire.

The city would have been cleared of the living. Then the dead from this quadrant, packed into transport that no longer needed owners, were sent on remote guidance into streets and parking buildings. Helicopters, also remotely controlled, were landing anywhere, atop each other. There would be more helicopters left than pilots.

This burning city was just one of many others destroyed to consume the dead. Morganna's voice now came on the sound-track, quiet and awed.

'Every quadrant in every country has one city like this. Some have more. The dead are taken there — the only practical means of destruction.'

It would be like that everywhere. I consciously detached myself, as though it were not real. No, Ciardh and my parents had not ended up like this, lifeless under thick smoke that covered everything like dark concrete. Darker shapes scudded across that smoke and my stomach crawled with icy horror.

More of those remote-controlled big-bellied helicopters were dropping into the thick fire-spotted smoke, immolating themselves like fat moths in candle-flame. The firestorm thrust up like a monster torch of achievement.

I did not watch this and the visuals cut; perhaps even Spoke could not watch anymore. Now a new voice, unfamiliar, came across, dispassionate and somehow as dead as those bodies.

'It's like that everywhere and no end in sight.'

The visuals were back at Spoke, at what used to be the main games hall. Now there were bunks and mattresses cluttered everywhere, with people on them. They were dressed in the light green utility-suits of Spoke and their faces were all spotted with black.

I knew none of the faces, and I was glad of that, because those black spots were a fungoid growth, sprouting to a thick ugly plait — out of head or body, eye, nose or ear.

The scene cut to that grey wall and yellow table where Morganna first talked to me.

'Blackroot got into Spoke — God knows how. Fifty per cent casualties, but contained.'

The speaker was a tall Asian with long black hair and dark smudges under his eyes. He rubbed his face and sounded very tired. KINSO was black-lettered on his tunic. 'We have perhaps nine months before we'll allow Earth to send up a shuttle. Enough time to get Protus in place —' So he thought he was talking to Shanto. 'What's happening on Mars may change the main plan but not much —'

The screen split-clicked and Shanto appeared, sitting on a bunk in the same faded tracksuit, flicking olives into the air around his mouth and gulping at them. A cynical smile was directed at me.

'You don't have to know that, Declan.' He tapped an olive with his fruit-knife, so that it bobbed into his mouth. 'Full brief after we release Protus. Then Earth can't touch us. Greenspit and Blackroot —' He broke off, his long humorous face becoming set. 'A second plague, Blackroot, not even a mutant. It's on Spoke and the population is down to thirty per cent. Listen, Declan.'

Shanto leant forward, his face serious. 'Keep *Copernicus* on course for the Protus launch. That's our priority. Earth's government is down to twenty-three nations. The others are practically non-existent because the plagues keep killing. But we can turn this around with Protus. So launch, Declan, launch! Update ends.'

This time the click-click was final and I pulled the scanner-goggles off. What the hell did Shanto mean? How could Protus make any difference after two plagues and massive casualties? How could technical data on Jupiter do anything for Earth? Both those plagues must have had incredible incubation periods to have struck Spoke. And we were months away from getting any data from Jupiter.

What the hell could Protus do?

All this was still a long dark tunnel; even my desperate scramble over the hull meant nothing compared with what I had just heard.

The intercom hummed. It was Belinda. 'Commander, I need to see you — alone.'

'Alright.' The intercom was open, so the others would be listening. I gave Belinda a moment to clear the cabin, then spoke again. 'Conception, any problems?'

'No.' She sounded as highly strung as ever.

'We want out —' This was Redgrove and I had no hesitation in cutting him off.

Belinda might be our killer, or she might be a rabid Stoner. So I stowed away the goggles and pulled the hand-laser from my pocket, sticking it into my wristband.

Belinda entered, her eyes opening wide as she saw the hand-laser.

'Commander?'

I shrugged, keeping my face blank. Whoever was over-riding our systems was an electronics master, and there was nothing on Belinda's file to suggest she was that.

'What is it you want? Do you really think —' She started to come closer but stopped as I put my hand over the laser. Despite the moment, she shot a fascinated glance outside. Jupiter was closer now, flushing a deeper red, it seemed.

She looked back at me, her lips moving as though uncertain how to frame her words. 'I've been running some data patterns,' she said. 'Random, but they all had a common factor. I think I know what's causing this.'

'You think? And do you know what's happened in the last hour?'

'Never mind the last hour.' Her square face was like a solemn, solid brick. 'We're all lucky to be alive. Because of Protus and our mission —' She paused, then came straight to the point. 'We have to destroy that thing.'

I brought the tank visuals up onscreen. Protus was swimming in its restless way, those luminous orbs lighting up the clear ruby fluid.

'Protus?' I asked. *What could she know?*

'I know what Simon found out. And Shanto —' She stopped with a little choke as though overcome with emotion, as though swallowing something. She was moving one hand and trying to speak again, her eyes bulging wide. One shaky finger pointed at Jupiter through the observation port. Her lips were moving and her face was pale with effort as she tried to speak.

Then, quite suddenly, she wasn't there.

She vanished. One moment she was standing there, her face an unnatural white, as though she'd been lightly dusted with fine powder. The next moment she disappeared into an even finer powder. Her boots remained and her utility-suit, and above the collar, just like Simon, there was the horrible dust-like suggestion of a human face. Like mist, like a hologram fading, it lightly drifted away.

With a sudden jar and a deadly chill, the air-filter systems came on and the fine dust was sucked away. Her tracksuit flapped as though in a mocking jog. My finger hit the alarm button.

Belinda was gone, like Shanto and Simon.

I have to rest for a little time now, as the pain is bad again. I need to be fully alert to tell you what Jupiter was like. And what happened in her oceans. And if I'd known what was ahead, maybe I would have let Jupiter's gravity wrench us into tiny pieces.

Because Belinda's death was the beginning of things more awful. Things that still hit me like a nightmare punch in the face.

End first transmission.

END FIRST VIS REC TRANSMISSION

The voice is rasping now, like it's always dry. I watch as my 'other self' crams another handful of those capsules into his mouth and gulps more water. The horror still holds me rigid. Elissa leans forward and sets the screen on hold, freezing that onscreen-Declan in the act of gulping water.

This still feels unreal. Taking that many capsules is practically a death-sentence in itself — my body could not sustain the impact, but somehow it has and I feel fine. 'Fine' is the wrong word. I feel shocked and numb. I have to start thinking. This was a lethal and hideous puzzle with too many unknown pieces.

'Elissa, personal check, life-signs, every cabin, okay?'

'Okay.' She goes out. The solid silent hush of the spaceship surrounds me. Behind the Moon was Earth, blue, white and green, looking normal. Communication systems were still downlined; I had a feeling they would stay that way until this Declan-transmission ended. I open the control locker to see if there are any clues there; there's one, a fully charged hand-laser, and I tuck it into my belt. I cannot trust Elissa, not yet.

Elissa slips into her chair and smiles. 'I checked and everyone's there. Shanto, Reliant, Redgrove, Simon, Belinda and Conception.' Rattling off the names, her smile is tense. 'All under cryo and doing fine.'

'Then I'm hallucinating?'

'Yes. The mission blotted out somehow but we're okay.'

'Let's see.'

What instinct of horror put those words into my mouth?

Elissa is looking at me as I fast-forward to the next vis-rec.

EIGHT

> *Onscreen-Declan's tired voice fills the flight-deck. As I listen, my flesh crawls again.*
>
> *'I know what you're thinking. You've checked cryo, everyone is there so this has to be a crazy dream — right?' He pauses, stretching that weary grin. 'I wish it was. But it's not.'*
>
> *'Of course it is,' snapped Elissa and, as though onscreen-Declan had heard her, he gives another weary grin.*
>
> *'It gets worse.'*

SECOND VIS REC TRANSMISSION BEGINS: I hit the alarm the instant Belinda vanished, opening the cabins, and suddenly everyone was on deck. Elissa tugged at Belinda's floating utility-suit, hooking her finger into the wrist-console strap and downlining the boots from the deck. She stuffed them into one of the control lockers and sat down.

Red Jupiter-light flickered off all our faces as she scanned again and checked the readouts. 'That same faint chemical trace again — like Simon. Somehow her body biodegraded into particles so fine that they went through our filter system.'

'A free-form hologram of some kind? Or Declan hallucinating?' Redgrove was frowning at me, suspicious as hell.

'A free-form hologram dressed in a utility-suit?' snapped Elissa, just ahead of me.

'An alien virus then.' Conception whispered the words, her eyes glittering.

'No data,' snapped Elissa, but not saying 'impossible'.

'Let's think about the Protus launch,' I said.

Outside, the orange mass of Jupiter was closer and the Red Spot was like an oval mouth, set to swallow us. That pulled the others together, got them thinking like a crew again. Jupiter is one planet that you just don't mess around with.

'Stations,' I said.

Elissa was beside me, Redgrove doubled for Belinda, and Conception went to the rear, standing in for Simon. On her own. I had to admire her for that. I wished it was Redgrove, because I did not like having him beside me.

Outside, the engines flared, holding us away from the pull of Jupiter's gravity. *Copernicus* shuddered slightly with the effort of holding course, the coils working at full blast. Redgrove could double as engineer and release Protus from aft-control. Even so, they all paused, watching me. They needed that direct order.

'We launch Protus. That's what we came here for.'

Easy to say. Not so easy to do.

Jupiter's surface gravity-pressure is twenty-five thousand tonnes per square millimetre. Translated, Jupiter will squash you flatter than a postage-stamp. The surface is methane and ammonia oceans and above that are clouds, hundreds of kilometres thick.

Through Protus we would be the first to see that 'surface'— a mixture of liquid hydrogen some fifteen thousand kilometres deep. Jupiter's gravity would squash the most solid metal out of existence. Protus's body was little more than solid jelly-matter. Nonetheless, it was perfectly adapted for life in those storming chemical oceans.

'We're introducing life to another planet,' came Conception's voice from the rear.

'Too late for ethics,' I replied.

There was no answer from Conception so I hoped she was satisfied. The hand-laser was still tucked in my belt, and I was unpleasantly aware that I might be sitting between two killers.

'In position for launch,' said Elissa. No answer from Conception. 'Launch countdown initiated.'

Now I had only seconds to decide. *Decide what?* To balance that vague disquiet and the hints about Protus against the success of this mission. Earth needed this success. Earth could handle Spoke, even on a bad day, and whatever Shanto had planned had died with him. I felt a stabbing pain in my stomach and I rubbed it hard. Cramp, that was all, and I leaned forward.

'Elissa, hold countdown.'

She looked at me. 'Declan, *twenty seconds!*'

'Then answer quickly!' I snapped back. 'Could Protus, in any way, have caused what happened — those vanishings?'

Elissa was rigid but she did answer quickly. 'No. Protus is a genetically engineered life-form, a mobile analysis-unit, not even fully activated.' Her voice rose in a tense pitch. 'Declan, *Copernicus* cannot stand this stress long, we must launch Protus. If it's causing problems, let's get *rid* of it!'

Copernicus was shuddering, jarring with the effort of staying in place. What Elissa said made sense.

'Launch Protus,' I said.

Now onscreen, the system-line cleared as *Copernicus* shuddered as though it had run into something invisible. Below us, splashing red fluid spread out in giant droplets. Through them glided Protus, suddenly launched from security into the unknown. Every new-born animal has natural instincts. The sudden change of temperature sent Protus an energising signal. Its stabilising fins spread like wings, skimming over the clouds and casting its shadow like a giant flying fish. Its instincts to survive guided it as it glided steeply into the icy silver-blue clouds.

'Those clouds are 150 degrees Celsius below freezing,' I said.

It was so cold that if Protus was not working it would freeze solid. The systems upscreened and Conception's voice came over, flat and unexcited. 'I'm getting stable readings.'

'Patch in visuals,' said Elissa.

The screen cleared and froze to an icy blue. Now, we were seeing through the 'eyes' of Protus. Plunging down and down, it was just a reddish-dark murk because very little light would penetrate those clouds. Protus was diving through like an animal sensing home and safety; alive and responding to the gentle touch of Elissa's fingers.

Elissa leaned forward intently. She and Shanto had been unlikely partners, pushed together by the various pressure-groups on Spoke. Now she was entranced, grinning like a kid.

Maybe she was a Stoner or the killer but I was suddenly glad she was second-in-command. She glanced at me, caught my smile, and went back to the visuals.

'When will Protus clear the cloud-cover?' I asked.

'Very soon.'

The visuals were still dipping and plunging deep into the murk. Soon we would see what nobody else had — the surface of Jupiter. That almost made up for the nightmare puzzle around us. Now, suddenly, the red-brown clouds cleared abruptly into a blue-dark atmosphere.

'Hell ...' breathed Elissa.

She did not say it as a swear-word, more as a wondering comment. Ahead, the view levelled out and slowed, as though the unnatural hellscape of Jupiter was a home that held no horrors.

Like the horrors still waiting to happen on *Copernicus*.

And the surface of Jupiter below cloud-level? See it yourself on the ship's visual data. My words cannot describe this new corner of our solar system. Glimpsing something unseen by humans since the dawn of time — just thinking about it choked me with awe. And knowing that more awesome secrets would be revealed when Protus went below the liquid surface.

Protus was developed from a deep-ocean fish who swam in blackness and was therefore accustomed to little or no light. But there was more light than expected beneath the clouds. The light came from immense forked streaks of angry blue lightning.

Now came sharp retorts that we could hear through the

ears of Protus, mixed with continuous booming rumbles of thunder, as though solid chunks of noise were rolling and grinding against each other.

And now came the ocean-surface of Jupiter.

The wave-pattern was so like Earth's that it was uncanny. But Earth's seas were not that frozen dark colour; nor did the waves rise to such mountainous peaks. They were liquid hydrogen, reflecting back the lightning streaks. And sometimes through the Protus-eye we glimpsed the little Protus-shadow on those storm-waves, alone but unafraid and trusting to instinct in that alien ocean. Did it sense it was a place of safety and security even though lightning crackled like a network of glowing, jagged bars around it?

'Lightning strike — is that possible?' I breathed.

'Don't even think about it,' Elissa breathed back.

Shanto would have loved this. But for now the deadly puzzle aboard *Copernicus* was forgotten as Protus dropped further and further into the dark primeval ocean-world.

Through the eyes of Protus we saw the waves reaching hundreds of kilometres into the air, tipped with icy hydrogen foam, the first fine mist splattering against Protus's eyes — so close that I blinked as though it were stinging my own eyes. Now Protus levelled for a first orbit before its descent into the oceans.

'On course and all systems fine.' Elissa smiled and all the tension went from her face; a good-looking face, I thought.

'Looks like we've got a live one,' I said.

It was a really weak joke but she smiled again and shook her head in wonderment. Incredibly, transfixed by that alien seascape, we had forgotten what was happening on the ship.

But the joke broke the spell. Her face closed and she leaned back in her chair with a sigh.

'So where do we go from here?' she asked.

Our flight schedule was clear enough. Protus would do one scanning orbit before plunging into the ocean. So far, its body was adjusting well to the pressure, but I ran another systems check. Everything was normal, Conception and Redgrove okay in the rear unit. Soon we would raise our orbit and begin the journey home. Elissa cut the intercom and looked at me.

'You went outside.'

She said it as a statement. As we watched Protus, she'd quietly onlined the systems log and seen the airlock registering as opened. Very clever. She'd not been as entranced as I'd thought.

'Yes. I thought Reliant might've had Shanto's disc.'

'Did she?' I shook my head, hoping it looked natural, and not expecting her next words.

'That took incredible guts, Declan.'

I just shrugged and onlined the intercom before the others became twitchy. Anyway, I had pushed those horrible struggling minutes to the back of my mind — it was that or freak out. Fear had driven me in that desperate time, not courage.

'We're on this orbit for ten hours,' I said, wanting to change the subject. We would ride cover on Protus for this one Jupiter day — the planet turned very fast on its axis. 'Then we break orbit and head for home.'

'And hope nobody else vanishes.' Redgrove's voice was as sarcastic as ever.

Elissa replied, her voice unexpectedly sharp. 'Redgrove,

none of us would have come this far without Declan. We've launched Protus, we still have a chance. Just once, stick your attitude where the sun doesn't shine.'

There was no answer from the intercom but I thought I heard Conception titter. It was good hearing Elissa put Redgrove down, but I had things to do: there was still data on Shanto's disc. That meant playing the bad-tempered, insecure commander again.

'Elissa, get into after-control with Redgrove and Conception. Finish that second flight-program. All three of you together ought to be okay.'

'And leave you alone? Like Simon and Shanto?'

'I'm like you, Elissa. I don't vanish easily.'

There was a curious and hesitant look in her eyes, as though she was not sure how to place me. I shifted in my seat as cramp stabbed through my side, and her face tightened. She'd seen the laser tucked in my belt. Now she scowled.

'Would you use that?'

'Would you?'

I pulled the laser out and flicked it towards her. It bobbed in the weightless air and Elissa swiped it aside. She gave me a furious look as she left the flight-deck, announcing her position at after-control a minute later. But already I wasn't listening. I had too much else to think about.

I gave them thirty minutes to settle down. Through the saucer-eyes of Protus came Jupiter's blue-dark surface flaring onscreen. Protus was gliding along, unaffected, as though it knew that this stormy alien jungle was its natural environment.

All systems were working. Protus was already transmitting through the Callisto booster, loud, clear and precise. In an hour it would be nearing the great Red Spot and that would be worth seeing. At any other time I would have been over-hyped; now, though, the magic was gone.

Maybe it had happened when Elissa slammed the laser aside. Of course she didn't know about the second laser tucked in my belt at the back, under my jacket. It was a cheap trick to see if she would use the laser — a tactic of desperation. But I still had not even a hint about who my unseen enemy was. All I did know was Shanto's big power play — and that somehow Protus was linked. Now Protus had gone into Jupiter's storm-charged atmosphere, and was it only my imagination or did the ship seem less oppressive and dominant?

Once again the rest of the crew were shut away. And it was time to see what else lay on the edited highlights of Shanto's disc. I was aware of how much my body ached as I settled on the scanner and those split-clicking lines shimmered around me.

The bleak office outlines of Spoke-control came into place. Two people were there and I knew one — Kinso, a bandage around his forehead. The other was a young woman with dark blonde hair in thick plaits. Straightaway, before either spoke, I knew that things were worse.

Much worse.

NINE

> *Elissa is beside me, one of Cybele Reliant's 'Amazons'. I'm still not certain I should trust her. But all of this is hitting her the same way it hits me. And nobody is dead, but onscreen-Declan thinks there is and that is somehow worse.*
>
> *Rebellion in Spoke, rebellion on Mars; colonies cutting away from a dying planet. Their high-tech, luxurious and ordered lives disrupted by violent death. Just as humans went from one continent to another, now from one planet to another.*
>
> *Onscreen-Declan, you know things I do not. About myself/ourself, about Elissa, who I feel drawn to but am scared of. Why am I feeling like this, with no memory but somehow on the edge of high adventure and great challenge? Keep talking ...*

The woman had RAHILDA black-lettered on her tunic — a technician, I thought, junior-grade engineer. Her eyes were red-rimmed and her face was pale.

'We are the last Spoke answering signals,' she said. 'The

others are mostly full of the dead, a few survivors fighting each other. Spoke Rhodes has been taken over by Stoners. Moon-Base has joined the rebels on Mars. Earth has cut our lines and we are under siege. But we can last out.'

Last out? How long did they think an orbiting Spoke *could* last out? Now it was Kinso who spoke, in a weary and low voice.

'There is a third plague on Earth. It's called "Red Dimmer". It kills by choking, very quickly. Earth may have only ten per cent of its population left after Red Dimmer runs its course. So we have opened communications with Moon-Base for federation talks.'

Communication! Federation! They were in *dreamland* — even if Earth was too busy to strike back. And there was a word for what they were really doing. The woman, Rahilda, came in now, voicing it easily enough.

'Treason? Yes, some on Spoke thought so too.' She glanced at Kinso; perhaps that bandage around his head meant there had been fighting. 'But with Protus we can make this work. Plague levels on Earth are still rampant, ash from all those burning cities is affecting the sunset. Earth must fight the plagues before they fight us, or the human population will fall below recoverable levels.'

'*Their* recoverable levels,' cut in Kinso. 'We know the answer to that, eh Shanto?' He was actually smiling as though the survival of our species was not important. 'Population centres too depleted, people going underground, law and order breaking down. But if the Protus mission succeeds, then that need not concern us.'

What did they think Protus could do? How could one biogenetic probe make so much difference? My hands twitched.

I wanted to somehow force myself into visual-reality and grab them by their stupid scheming necks, both so smugly detached from the holocaust on Earth.

Rahilda was speaking now. 'Red Dimmer or not, our schedule remains the same. Launch Protus, complete the planet orbit and —' Rahilda broke off. She was looking at Kinso, who had suddenly stiffened in his seat. Both hands were flat on the table and his cheeks were puffed out. He stood up, shaking, his mouth open. He gasped, jerked his head, his face darkening to a horrible black-red. Then, half-turning, he threw his body against the table and slid limply out of sight.

All of this happened in moments. Rahilda stayed where she was, sharp though, and knowing exactly what had happened to Kinso, knowing also that she could not escape, because his death was a dreadful truth.

Red Dimmer had come to Spoke.

'Shanto,' she said, 'we're not going to make it.' I had to admire her courage, because even then her body twitched as the virus took hold. 'All Spoke may be dead before you get back. So you and your creatures have won.' Her face was suffusing with that red-dark shadow, her voice gasping. 'So you're the Lord of Creation — or so you think — but you'll outsmart yourself, you evil —'

The last words shot out as she jerked in her seat and doubled over across the table. It was awful to watch but the screen zap-clicked at that moment.

So Red Dimmer was on Spoke and I had seen how fast it worked. That was months and months ago, of course; all of Spoke Carthage would be dead by now. Rahilda's last word was uttered with such force — *evil*.

Shanto had appeared again, *smiling* — as though the violent deaths did not matter. He was leaning back on his bunk, his legs crossed. 'Some things I will tell you myself, Declan. You'll be waking up from cryo-sleep soon. This is to give you the broad picture. And think, Declan, because you can when you try. And listen.'

He leaned forward and with a little push floated himself up into the air over his bunk. He spat something out of his mouth and I realised it was olive pits. Shanto had some disgusting habits.

'We are talking about control, Declan. The high ground of space — therefore of world systems. And, you are asking yourself, has Shanto spaced out? Excuse the pun.'

He grinned again and flicked another olive into his mouth. 'Declan, there is proto-life in Jupiter's oceans that we can use. So even mass deaths on Earth and Spoke don't matter. What does matter is Protus swimming in those oceans. All will be explained soon.'

His virtual-reality image took no notice of my yelled 'Shanto!' and the screen clicked. I took the scanner off as Elissa came online. She had heard me yell over the intercom.

'Declan?'

'Just thinking aloud.'

I checked the disc readout. It had ended, and there would be nothing more. Sometime after that, too-clever Shanto had been stabbed to death in his cabin and I still had no answers.

And why did the plagues not matter? And what did Rahilda's dying words mean: *you and your creatures*? No answers, *still* no answers. All I had left were clever word-games and a Renaissance hologram.

Elissa's voice came again. 'Declan —'

'I'm okay!' I snapped. 'Cool down!'

'Cool down?' she shouted. 'Check your Protus visuals — we're headed for disaster!'

I tore off the scanner and upscreened. That blue-dark seascape was exploding into full view and another crash of forked lightning split a jagged line down the screen. I was again looking through Protus's eyes. Ahead, as our view uptilted, there was another stunning reminder of Jupiter — and the disaster we were headed for.

The Red Spot.

Now it was not just a red mark on Jupiter's surface. It was a raging and storming gigantic red mass, *three times* the size of Earth. It tore up from the storm-tossed hydrogen ocean, spouting into a massive red tornado trunk, jetting a monstrous pillar of storming energy.

'Everyone, flight-deck.'

They all came, very quickly. And like me, they just watched, because that mega-huge upthrust pillar was just too awesome. The top was capped in red, methane or sulphur, the rest of it pure hydrogen. Elissa spoke quietly and precisely. 'Protus cannot take that turbulence. It will be torn to pieces.'

Redgrove could not possibly miss this chance to sneer. 'So which genius planned a collision with the Red Spot?'

Elissa upscreened her readouts. 'A Spoke program. The Spot does move, you know.'

'Can you stop Protus?' I asked.

Elissa's voice had a new edge — despair. 'Shanto had the codes.'

Shanto had the codes. Great! Nine months of deep-space

voyage then danger and death. All for a bird's-eye view of Protus slamming into that tornado and being torn into gelatine ribbons.

'We can't let this happen.' My words sounded futile.

Conception spoke from the flight-deck entrance. 'We can't stop it. It's too close.' Her voice dropped to a whisper, sounding a note of ... was it joy? 'Protus will be sucked in like something down a plughole.'

I had only a few minutes, scarcely enough time to cross wits with Galileo, let alone tell the others that I could voice-ac the ship's systems.

'Galileo?'

They all gaped at me then looked past me to the hologram-receiving points, to the sudden appearance of a tall grey-bearded man in a long brown robe, who looked at them without a flicker of interest, as though they were street-urchins in the muddy alleys of Renaissance Italy. By now, I knew the protocol.

'Signore Galilei, this is Elissa, Redgrove and Conception.'

He bowed, but a little deeper to Conception. 'A good Italian name,' he said.

'Shanto's bloody holograms,' Redgrove breathed.

Galileo looked at Redgrove and opened his mouth to rebuke this discourtesy. I cut in quickly. 'Galileo, we have to divert Protus from a storm-centre. You must pass on a message to dive early.'

Galileo frowned and cracked his big bony knuckles. There was utter silence on the flight-deck as the others still gaped at him. Of course he loved being the centre of attention. You could see it, even in the way he finally shook his head, his voice firm but apologetic. 'I cannot see a way.'

Then unexpectedly he smiled at Conception. 'Yes, a lovely name. I nearly gave it to one of my daughters. I called her Arcangela instead. Both of my daughters became nuns.'

'With your blessing?' I asked.

I received a sharp look from Elissa and a muttered 'I don't believe this' from Conception. But I *knew* Galileo now. Question and answer. Let him lead the conversation.

'Hey, this is crap!' shouted Redgrove.

Even he shut up at a look from Galileo. The old boy sat on his little stool, the laboratory clutter around him, oblivious to the raging stormscape on our screens or Protus skimming over those hydrogen wave-tips to destruction.

'Of course, my daughters were born out of wedlock,' he said. Was that a slightly embarrassed catch to his voice? 'As they say, bastard slips cannot take root.'

'Did you want them to be nuns?' I glared at the others to shut them up.

Galileo shrugged again. 'Oh, they could not marry. But youth can only be advised, not directed.'

'Bloody hell!' yelled Redgrove. 'Our mission is cracking up and the ship's computer is giving us a lecture on morality.'

'My dear young man,' said Galileo, offended, and abruptly downlined.

I yelled for him to come back online. He didn't. Was that offended dignity? Or had he said everything he intended to?

'So what was that all about?' asked Elissa, still looking at the empty console points in fascinated wonder.

'He leaves clues in his conversation,' I said.

'So what particular clue did we get?' snapped Redgrove, scowling. 'Considering it's three minutes to impact.'

'A clue?' Elissa set her face in thought. 'Illegitimate daughters ... bastard slips?'

'Illegitimacy, against the laws of creation,' said Conception softly, her eyes on the screen.

'Yeah, and children not listening to their fathers,' said Redgrove sarcastically. 'Two minutes and nothing that old screwball said is any help.'

We looked at that closing storm-face through Protus's scanning eye. Protus, innocently intent, was heading for destruction and so was our mission. But a feeling grew inside me, from Galileo's booming voice, as though keys were waiting for locks.

Beside me, Elissa was compiling a search-pattern of what Galileo had said. She wasn't giving up, so I couldn't. Let Redgrove mutter and Conception sulk. What Galileo said — children not listening to their parents. *No.* Galileo didn't say that. He said only that children can be *advised*!

Protus was Shanto's child. A child to be advised?

Redgrove was jabbering about something, but he shut up when I spoke aloud. 'Galileo, I know you can hear me. Pass this on to Protus.' Someone hissed with incredulity but I ignored that. I took a deep breath, thought quickly and spoke firmly.

'Protus, you are Shanto's creation. I am Commander Declan Tulropper, giving you a direct order ... no, advice. Forget Shanto's program. You are in life-threatening danger and he cannot help. You must go sub-surface otherwise you will be destroyed, repeat destroyed!'

Nothing happened. The massive hydrogen spout was closer, and Protus was skimming towards it in blind faith. Unhearing or uncaring of what I had said. But I went on, because something more than simple instinct was telling me to.

'Well, your pet hologram didn't pass it on,' said Conception, actually sounding happy.

'Protus!' I yelled. 'You don't know what to believe but I am giving you good advice. Shanto is gone. Go under!'

Now the screen was full of dark storms, and Protus rushing madly at that full tornado spout. 'Protus, I am trying to help —'

Copernicus jarred and the light dimmed. Suddenly — readouts accelerating — our spaceship was shaking and shuddering. Redgrove and Conception were standing, and the shockwave was so powerful that their boots broke contact with the deck and they floated up, arms and legs flailing comically.

But there was nothing comical about it. *Copernicus* was power-surging as though every system was raging on overload. And through it, through the noise, came an almost-unheard whispering, the words inaudible. And onscreen, the Jupiter seascape was shifting. Conception was pointing and screaming.

'It's turning!'

It was! Now the rushing storm-centre was shifting over as our Protus-eye view angled away. Below, the dark skimming shadow flickered over white hydrogen wave-tips, the shapes changing as it angled. Now the wave-tips grew closer and closer and Elissa gasped.

'It heard you. It's going in!'

Protus was going in, and quickly. Angling sideways as though suddenly sensing the danger, it dived more deeply, a wave-top splashing directly beneath it. A brief plunging moment into the toppling side of a wave, a splash of dense hydrogen, and abruptly Protus went under.

So sharply it went, the pure white surge of hydrogen so complete and realistic around us, that I blinked. I forgot all our nightmares for that incredible moment because Protus was safe under the seas of Jupiter. Silence. I think that only I heard the faint unseen click of knuckles. Galileo had been watching too.

Elissa spoke as though not quite believing her words. 'Protus is working, all systems going. It's adjusting, adapting to the new chemical density.' Her voice rose in pitch. *'It's working!'*

The ship's systems were still jarring and shuddering, the noise-blast seeming to come from inside and outside. Loud and rushing, tearing at my mind, those inaudible words came again. Like baby-words, like an expression of relief as the onscreen visuals blanked.

Conception had grabbed the top of a chair to pull herself down. She set her boots to full pressure and they clanged into place. Her face was flushed as she looked at us. 'What happened?'

'Protus is re-adjusting vision-scanners,' said Elissa. 'It'll come online when it's fully compensated for the different density.' She leaned back in her chair and looked at me. 'You talked to Protus.'

'Yes, and made that giant-sized mackerel understand him.' Redgrove had come down behind me. 'How long have you been able to do that?'

'Just a guess, from what Galileo said,' I replied.

'Galileo — oh yes!' Redgrove's voice was as unpleasant as ever. 'And when were you planning to mention *him*?'

'Yes, when we'd all vanished?' snapped Conception. 'Do you know what's causing *that*?'

Why crew-members were vanishing? Yes, I had the smallest, half-formed idea about that too. So I hesitated for a fatal moment and they read it in my face. I shook my head and spoke quickly. 'I don't know.'

'We think you do,' said Elissa slowly. 'Certainly more than you're telling us.'

I didn't register right then. Later, I worked out that they must have planned this in after-control. When I shut the intercom to stop them listening, I also stopped myself hearing. They had planned this, even down to Redgrove getting behind me. And even wondering if I had a second laser. Redgrove pulled it neatly from my waist-band. I didn't have to look around to know he was pointing it at my head.

'You are all over-reacting,' I said.

'Are we?' returned Elissa smoothly. 'But Declan, we do know more than you cared to tell us.'

So it was a mistake to leave them together like that. Elissa explained all this, her words as smooth (and cold) as her face. While I had the virtual-reality scanner on, they had patched the ship's systems and seen it too. They had known since the hull-walk that I was playing a different game.

Everything Shanto, Morganna, Kinso and Rahilda had said to me, they also knew. But not (said Elissa quickly) who tried to kill me. They were all in different parts of the spaceship at the time.

'Earth, plagues, the rebels on Spoke!' yelled Conception suddenly. 'We had the right to know about them!'

'Commander, we must discuss this,' said Elissa. 'Until then, you are confined to quarters.'

Even with Redgrove shoving a laser in my ear, I was not going to make things easy. One of them might be my killer. 'Back on Spoke, I will have your commissions for this.'

'Spoke is gone, maybe Earth too,' said Redgrove and pushed the laser hard to my head.

'What about Jupiter?' I said to Elissa, sensing that she was the ringleader. 'We're not free of the planet or her moons.'

'I can fly *Copernicus*.' Even so, she hesitated before giving her first order. 'Put him in his cabin.'

'Not his cabin,' said Redgrove, ever-pleasant. He was just longing to use that laser. 'Too many systems.'

And, being Redgrove, he'd already worked out where to put me. The others agreed, Conception at once, Elissa (I was glad to note) a little more reluctantly. Even so, I made them force me out of the command chair. And I glared at them all. Just so long as they knew what they were doing.

We were all in deep space but they were all in very deep water. Releasing Protus was a first. So, in a manner of speaking, was this.

The first mutiny in space exploration.

TEN

> *Another pause and onscreen-Declan leans back. These pauses are becoming longer and more frequent. There's a dead whiteness to his skin now but some spark is keeping him going. Something that he has to tell Elissa and myself.*
>
> *The other cryo-systems are lock-coded to the end of this transmission. We can't transmit or receive for the same reason. He's gone to a lot of trouble to make sure we listen.*
>
> *And I should be distrusting Elissa now. She led a mutiny back there. But I don't. More and more it's like we're partners and I even want to reach out and hold her hand. Assurance? As this tale of horror gets more horrible, I need assurance.*

Yes, Redgrove knew where to put me. It was clever when you think about it. The tank had housed Protus for nine moths so it was obviously secure. I could breathe through the old filtration systems, even though it was very cold. All of deep space had flooded inside when the tank drained. Streaks of that red support-fluid had turned the floor to ruby glass. Ruby fragments of ice tinkled from overhead.

Redgrove and Conception waited at the door as Elissa followed me inside. They were keeping each other in sight at all times. Elissa knocked on the thick glass. 'We'll patch the intercom through to your wrist-unit so you can follow what's happening.'

'Some heating would be nice.'

'Let him stay on ice,' said Conception. 'Might help him remember more about Shanto's murder.'

Some fragments of the red ice tinkled around me as she spoke; a little piece of the puzzle fell suddenly into place.

'Murder weapon?' I pointed up at the ceiling of the tank.

When Protus was released into Jupiter-orbit, the red fluid was mostly ejected with it. But whatever was left froze at once, some of it in long icicles hanging from the ceiling, like thin red daggers. With the warm air coming in, they detached and fell to the floor.

'Shanto was playing with a fruit-knife,' I said. 'It stayed floating and punctured his overhead cryo-lines. So after he delivered his message and went back into cryo, the same thing happened. An ice-dagger formed and as the cabin warmed —' I made a downward-jabbing movement with my thumb.

'No wonder there was no murder weapon,' breathed Elissa. 'It melted into water vapour.'

The others believed it too: a simple accident because Shanto had been too clever for himself, too deep in his complex power-games. His vision of tomorrow had been ended by a stray fruit-knife.

Elissa backed to the door. 'That doesn't explain the disappearances. Or why Reliant was on the hull.' She motioned the others back. 'Until we have some answers, you stay here.' The door shut.

Even now the tank was warmer; the thick red fluid thawing on the floor had a fleshy smell and was sticky underfoot. A moment later my wrist-console came to life and Elissa's cool voice with it. She said that we were still leaving orbit and ahead now was Io.

Io. Think of a surface like a giant yellow and red pizza. Maybe the youngest surface in the solar system, it was constantly being reworked by sulphur volcanos. I grinned and spoke into the console. 'Redgrove, keep clear of Io. Some of those eruptions go more than a hundred k's into the air.'

'I know that!' came the instant retort. 'Think I'm stupid?'

'Yes.'

I think Elissa snickered as he offlined. I wished I could see Io that close. All those Galilean moons were nearly as big as Earth itself. Then I flinched as knuckles cracked suddenly and a loud voice boomed though the cabin.

'I was a schoolmaster once. A long step I took, as far as the heavens, to become the world's foremost astronomer.'

'What the hell are you doing here!'

The words jumped out, before I noticed the hologram-receiving points, almost hidden by their coating of red slime. Galileo was on his stool, playing with something that looked like a sheet of lead rolled into a short tube. His eyebrows lifted, his lips already forming a 'downline' as I hastily remembered my manners.

'Signore Galilei, an honour, the more so that it is unexpected.'

Galileo simply nodded, with a lofty twitch of his eyebrows. That rolled-lead tube was his telescope, for sure. 'I have endured prison — eight years — for daring to suggest that the Earth revolved around the sun.'

'Yes, but what do you want?'

The eyebrows met and the tone became severe. 'Young man, it is a great honour to be addressed by the world's foremost astronomer.'

And foremost ego-tripper, I thought. 'Weren't several astronomers ... ah ... foremost at the time?' And before them all, the Pole, Nicolaus Copernicus, who we named our ship after.

Galileo waved aside my trivial words. 'Some. Johannes Kepler, Tycho Brahe, Harriot the Englishman and —' he stopped speaking for a moment and his long fingers slid together — 'Giordano Bruno ...'

I let him speak. Everything he said was programmed; he'd come online for a Shanto-reason that would show itself in word play.

'Before me, Bruno dared believe the same. The Inquisition called it blasphemy. They ... they nailed his tongue with an iron spike and burned him at the stake. They only imprisoned me.'

'You were lucky.'

'I was very lucky.'

His voice shook a little. This scene was unreal. Galileo's hologram-presence burned into the red-dripping gloom of the Protus tank, everything silent around us. I offlined my wrist-console. At this moment Elissa and the others could do what they liked with *Copernicus*. Fear in Galileo's voice meant that we were getting somewhere. Shanto's hidden messages tended to come out with emotion. Shanto, of course, was a master at playing emotion.

'The Church taught that Earth was the centre of creation; the sun and other planets revolved around us.' I knew that much about our early history. 'So anything else was heresy? How did that explain the movement of the stars, then?'

Galileo gave a bitter chuckle. 'The stars? Oh, they were upon a giant winch system, wound around the Earth every twenty-four hours by an angel. That all changed when I looked through my telescope.' He gave a modest cough. 'The first of its kind.'

Get the conversation back to Jupiter! 'And you discovered the Galilean moons?'

'Yes!' His brown eyes blazed with pride. 'And how they rotated! Harriot and Kepler explored the cosmos, but *I* first proved the motion of the planets!'

'And you've come online to help us now?' I asked.

Wrong move! He just stroked his beard and gave a crafty smile. I would have to be a lot smarter than that. Draw him out. What else had he done?

'And you defined the laws of gravity.'

'Indeed.' He placed the telescope carefully on a shelf. 'From atop the leaning tower of Pisa, I dropped balls of gold, ebony, copper and porphyry.'

'Different densities but they all fell at the same speed?' He nodded solemnly and I just had to prick that ego-bubble a little. 'But every kid knows that now.'

'In my time, the greatest minds in science did not!' he snapped. 'Nor could they realise a simple truth — that ignorance of motion is ignorance of nature. *That* I also discerned from Jupiter's moons. One January morning in 1610.'

And that's something else every kid knows, I nearly said, but didn't. He'd finished speaking as though he'd been delivering a message. He picked up those little glass scales and tapped them. They swayed up and down. Then he gave his crafty smile and faded back to electronic limbo.

I sat thinking, still shivering a little. The floor was mucky and that red fluid stank. More lateral thinking. Was there something in the way he tapped those scales? Each end balancing the other. Ignorance of nature ... ignorance of motion.

Jupiter's moons! Ignorance of motion!

I operated my wrist-console to open the intercom. 'Elissa, are we still clearing orbit?'

Her voice came back, strained. 'No, we're slightly inside.' And of course she was too proud to ask for help. 'We're passing Ganymede.'

Motion! 'Elissa, re-adjust!' I yelled. 'You're way out. You haven't allowed for the gravitational tug between Europa and Ganymede. You'll get pulled too close!'

An error, a stupid kid's error. Mine too. I should've foreseen it! *Copernicus* shuddered and I could imagine Elissa hauling frantically on the main control, the burners flaring as she used our precious fuel reserves to pull us clear of that deadly gravitational trap.

The onscreen visuals patched through to my console points showed the pitted blue-silver surface of Ganymede coming closer with frightening speed. Then *Copernicus*, using all her engine-power, lifted and broke clear from that fatal orbit lock. There was a loud sigh of relief from Elissa.

'Thank you, Galileo,' I said in a low clear voice, certain that the old boy would hear it. Then, more loudly at the intercom, 'Okay, when you guys have finished proving how well you can fly a spaceship, you might like to check on Protus. It should be deep enough by now.'

Redgrove's angry two-word response made me grin. Then I thought of those visuals, maybe patched through by Galileo. *And* console points in the Protus-tank? The points could work in a fluid state, but what was Shanto teaching a barely sentient probe organism?

Now the console-points flickered again, patching the flight-deck visuals through. The screen was suddenly bathed in bright shifting bands of colour, a light orange mass shifting into dark, and through this swirled constantly changing patterns of red and yellow.

'It's working,' came Conception's awed voice.

Protus was alive and swimming in Jupiter's hydrogen ocean. Under extreme conditions, hydrogen becomes metal, but just above that — where Protus was now — it was liquid. So Protus — *swimming, alive* — had adjusted to a pressure of *five thousand million* tonnes per square metre.

Our problems were forgotten a moment. We were watching with Protus's saucer eyes as it glided and swooped on currents of liquid hydrogen, methodically quartering the ocean. It had endless thousands of years to complete its task. Shanto had even thought that Protus could assimilate the primitive carbons from this chemical ocean to restore its body structure indefinitely.

'You know there's methane and ammonia mixed with the hydrogen,' came Conception's voice. 'But I can't work out the analysis. It keeps changing.'

Suddenly, instead of that tight fretwork of swirling currents, a pale orange calm area appeared on the screen, as though Protus had swum into a storm-free sector. But a calm centre in an ocean of turbulence?

My first thought was that it must be a reverse whirlpool of some kind. Now there were tiny red dots appearing and Conception could not analyse those either. They were probably chemicals — perhaps a concentrated sulphur. Even down here in my prison I was fascinated.

'What are those red dots?' asked Elissa, on the intercom, to the others. Then she remembered me. 'Declan, any ideas?'

'Your guess is as good as mine,' I replied, trying not to sound sour.

Onscreen, that pale orange seemed endless. Protus glided on and on, the colours swimming past, our view angled as Protus began plunging down. Whatever this calm spot was, it was deep. More of the red spots appeared, bright as specks of blood.

'Still can't get a readout,' came Conception again.

You have to ask the right questions to get the right answers, I thought. Because even though it was fantastic and impossible, I guessed what those red spots might be. I was debating whether to tell them, when *Copernicus* shuddered again and Elissa yelled, 'I said *five* degrees!'

'I went *five* degrees!' yelled Redgrove back.

It appeared that crew unity was cracking. I knew what was happening and it was time to intervene. 'Elissa, you're still way too close to Ganymede. The planetoid's gravity is pulling us back.'

'We compensated!' she said loudly.

'And for Europa?'

'Yes, and we're still losing way!' This was Redgrove.

'I think you need me and Galileo,' I said quietly, and some hushed whispering broke out. Then Elissa spoke.

'Cleared to come up, Declan.' 'Declan', I noticed, not 'Commander'.

The tank hatch slid open and I went up. This was going to be tricky.

ELEVEN

None of them looked at me as I came in. They were hostile — even sulky. And they had good reason to be, as they had nearly piloted *Copernicus* to disaster. The commander's chair was free, but only so Redgrove could stand behind me with the laser.

Ganymede and Europa were behind us. Their gravitational pull had been much stronger than we thought. I looked at the readouts and, yes, we were still off-course. All three of them just looked at me in silence.

'Galileo?' I said aloud.

He appeared. He was actually trimming his beard with a pair of small scissors and a polished steel mirror. He glanced over, one bristly eyebrow raised at the sight of Redgrove's laser. But he was not surprised — Shanto would have programmed even for this.

'Galileo,' I said, 'I am passing voice-ac to Elissa. You may converse with her.'

'Young man, I may converse with whomever I please.' He examined his reflection in the mirror. 'The question is, may they converse with me?'

'Why not?' snapped Redgrove. 'You're part of the ship's system, that's all.'

I winced. Galileo would *love* that. Elissa cut in quickly and — using her good sense — politely. 'Galileo —'

'*Signore Galilei*, my girl.'

Girl. Elissa saw my grin. She set her mouth a moment then went on. 'There has been a change in command. Declan is no longer —'

She broke off as Galileo held up one hand, complete with scissors. 'I am not interested in petty squabbles.' And he downlined.

I winced again, this time concerned. Redgrove's laser was at my head and this petty squabble could get my brains burned out. To prove it, Conception pulled out her own laser. Her voice grated and she spoke tensely, sucking in breath between each sentence.

'So this ship is being run by smart-ass Declan and a Renaissance hologram?' Her eyes glittered. 'So let Galileo think about this! Who does his bloody high-and-mightiness talk to after Declan gets his brains fried?'

'Conception!' shouted Elissa.

'I will count to three!' She came up to me and Redgrove obligingly stepped back. 'One … two …'

'Committees are tedious,' boomed that well-known voice. Galileo was back, still trimming his beard, apparently not concerned that two lasers were pointed at me. 'Once I could not persuade a group of eminent scientists to look through my telescope and see the moons of Jupiter. Can you imagine such blinkered thinking? They simply could not see what was in front of them.'

Conception spoke first, pushing her laser into my ear. 'Galileo, we want voice-ac and intelligent bloody conversation, not riddles.'

I cut in, not daring to let Galileo reply. One dismissive answer would be one too many. 'Galileo, you can voice-copy to Elissa.'

'To all of us!' screeched Conception. She was highly stressed, very scared, and her hand was shaking. I was a twitch away from death.

'I am now voice-copied to Elissa,' said Galileo. 'She may include you if she chooses.'

His brown eyes rested on me and one eyelid flickered. Was it a wink? With a little smile on those bearded lips, he downlined again.

Silence. Elissa reached out and steadily pushed Conception's laser from my neck. Just as steadily she took it from Conception's shaking hand. 'Galileo is right,' she said. 'We can't fly by committee.'

'You're not giving us voice-ac?' shouted Redgrove.

Let them fight, I thought, then suddenly Galileo's wink and his last words came into my mind. *What was in front of them!* I looked at Jupiter's ocean, onscreen, and pointed: 'Can anybody explain *that*?'

Conception was still stressed, her eyes burning. But even she turned with the others, all of them looking at our view of Protus on the console screen.

That view was changing. The bio-probe was still in that strange calm area. More of the red spots still floated around. But now the coordinates changed as Protus circled and went deeper. It made a wide circle, about a kilometre, so that calm spot was obviously very wide. And it went plunging down, down, into the orange-red calm.

I was uneasy. Peace in the storming ocean was unnatural, just about impossible. The same unnatural feeling reflected around us. Why was Protus off-course? What had it sensed? What was it looking for?

'It's not on a straight course anymore,' muttered Redgrove. 'Some kind of malfunction?'

Elissa shook her head. 'Bio-readouts are fine.'

I spoke as quietly and casually as I could. 'We should get readouts on that stuff Protus is swimming in.'

It was enough to set Conception off again. 'You don't give orders! Who the hell —'

'He's right,' snapped Elissa. She had slipped into command-mode quickly. 'You and Redgrove run them through.'

'Yes, Commander, at once, Commander,' he responded mockingly. 'By the way, what are we looking for?'

'Anything that cross-matches,' she answered, with a look at me. 'Micro-analysis of those little red spots?'

'Something you should have done much earlier,' I said — under my breath, but from the angry look she shot me, she'd heard.

'Shut up or we'll stick you back in the tank.'

This was something Redgrove was good at. There was silence as he upscreened the readouts and cross-matched data. The mixing lines of data came together and Conception hissed, still as twitchy as hell. Redgrove looked at his data, not able to believe what he was seeing onscreen.

'Single-celled life-forms?' I said. 'At a guess?'

Conception's sharp cry sounded like the twang of a taut guitar. 'Life-forms ... intelligent?'

'What's the word ... protoplaza ...' muttered Redgrove.

'Those things are grouping like they're trying to form multiple-celled life.' He shook his head. 'That's impossible. Life can't begin in hydrogen and methane.'

'Not life as we know it,' said Elissa slowly. She would know, better than anyone, as she'd studied bio-genetics with Shanto. Now she frowned, trying to find the right words. 'This life-form is so ... so different and basic ... that it doesn't even know it's living yet.'

'That calm patch,' I said. 'Maybe it's some kind of pre-life soup. Maybe that's why Protus is taking an interest.'

'Yes, programmed to adjust its analysis for abnormalities.' Elissa nodded, the incredulous wonder still showing on her face.

The onscreen movement continued. Protus was still circling, as though fascinated. Earth had once had this kind of life, in oceans very much like those of Jupiter. Over millennia, our oceans cooled and complex life formed. But no Protus swam in our oceans.

'Hey!' cried Redgrove, all the mockery gone. 'I'm getting some kind of a power-surge.'

Elissa looked at her own console and I looked at mine. 'Growing stronger,' she said. 'Hell, the Callisto booster is picking it up too.'

She paused as our readouts flickered crazily. Through the spaceship came a sudden thrumming, vibrating sound. It seemed to thrill around us like emotion, like super-charged electronic adrenalin.

'What the hell is that?' whispered Conception.

Everyone was silent, feeling the tension of the unknown. The red Jupiter-light bathing the gleaming flight-deck now seemed baleful, glaring with a mysterious, mocking power.

'Growing stronger!' cried Redgrove. 'What the hell is it?'

'Something's getting into our systems, maybe,' said Elissa. 'A natural power-source from Jupiter, transmitted via Protus? Is that possible, Declan?'

'Unlikely.'

This power-force was probing, testing, even tuning our systems as though flexing a new muscle. I think Conception guessed at the same moment I did and abruptly downlined her console.

'Alright, let's get rid of Protus!'

'You're crazy!' shouted Elissa. 'Protus is the reason for our mission. Anyway, we couldn't; there's no destruct signal.'

'There must be a way,' Conception shouted back. 'We can cut off the Callisto booster — overload it and scramble Protus's memory-banks.'

Elissa had thought the tension was over before, and she'd foolishly put her hand-laser down by her console. Now Conception snatched it up, her face tinted and her eyes glittering with Jupiter-light. There was utter silence. Even the power-surge stopped, as though it was listening.

Conception stepped back to cover us all with her laser. Her voice was full of wild passion. 'I'm going to zap our ship's systems. We are not meant to be here!'

'Zap them and you zap us too!' shouted Elissa, her eyes wide with horror.

Conception just grinned, her eyes lit now with red madness. 'Yes, we must all die. Our punishment for infecting Jupiter as we infected our own planet.'

And now even Redgrove was getting the message. He swung around in his chair, incredulous. 'You're a Stoner, aren't you?'

'Yes, I'm a Stoner.' Conception's grin stretched over her white teeth. 'And right now I'm going to stop Protus damaging another planet's integrity! We will all die but so will Protus —'

'Conception!' screamed Elissa.

Maybe she knew what was going to happen. I did, with a horrible chilling certainty. Because Conception choked on that last word. Her mouth was still open but no more sound came. Her skin went white, prickling into a fine dust-mould of her features; even her hair went white and her hand, holding the laser. Then all of it vanished.

The weapon hung suspended. Her tracksuit, one empty sleeve extended, bobbed and deflated. Her boots remained stuck firmly to the floor.

Around us, the ventilation systems suddenly came to life. With ghostly ease, the remaining traces of her body vanished like a wafting spirit. In some two or three seconds of real time she was completely gone, just like the others.

At least, I thought, nobody could blame me this time.

TWELVE

> *'You did check each cabin, physically check?'*
>
> *'Yes, Declan.' Elissa's reply is terse and she scowls.*
>
> *Onscreen-Declan has paused again and I upscreen each cabin for a visual inspection. I do believe Elissa, and now I believe the evidence of my eyes. Simon, Belinda, Conception, all there. Is the real Conception a Stoner or is that as much a nightmare as the rest of this story?*
>
> *Onscreen-Declan seems to be gathering for a last effort. And he still manages that ghastly grin, because he knows how puzzled, how incredulous, we are. His voice is croaking all the time now but is still clear.*

They put me back in the Protus-tank. I suppose I would have done the same. The intercom was off and they didn't know I could work the screen. I knew exactly what they were doing. Elissa confirmed it an hour later when she came down the steps, the laser pushed in her belt.

She sat on the bottom step and ran a hand wearily

through her hair. 'Conception and the others ... some kind of new plague?'

'We'd all be dead.'

'I read her personal diary. Stoners believe that the plagues are virus mutations, the result of genetic experiments, cloning, chemicals in our food, radiation in our tele-channels. That the viruses can somehow transmit through our systems and regenerate at the other end, and that's how it got to Spoke. Possible?'

'Anything's possible.'

'They also say that these plagues were anticipated. That they're a useful way of cutting down the world population and keeping resource levels up. Could people think like that? Let that happen?'

I opened my mouth then shut it again. Shanto had talked about 'millions of unnecessary people' and the future needing only a small elite. That made me think of Ciardh and my parents. I went over and sat on the step beside Elissa and pointed.

Her gaze followed my finger and she sat up. 'The console points — in here?' She looked at me. 'Why —' She broke off, quick-witted, realising the implications.

'Right,' I said. 'When Protus went into Jupiter, it was already a lot smarter than we thought. And it knew our ship systems better than we did.'

Taught everything by Shanto — and Galileo. Elissa onlined the console and the big screen flicked into life. Protus was questing deeper still into that calm orange. More of those red dots floated now, like our own single-celled ancestors.

'I notice you haven't mentioned Protus,' I said.

'Meaning?' She glanced at me sharply.

She wasn't stupid though. She knew exactly what I was talking about. She and Redgrove would have scanned and re-scanned and they would know that constant factor now.

'Meaning that people who take too much interest in Protus tend to vanish.'

She threw me another sharp look, then she sighed and nodded. Simon had been scanning Protus when *he* went. Belinda had discovered something — maybe the secret intelligence. Conception had been about to shoot out our console link with Protus.

'Do you think that Protus is causing this?' she asked.

There was a careful and neutral tone to her voice and I replied in the same way. 'Or someone controlling Protus — someone who can override systems. Someone smart enough to hide from our scans.'

'Shanto?' Elissa shook her head. 'Something very sharp punctured his heart and that's as dead as you get. Anyway, I can't think of anything that just makes people disappear.'

A yell interrupted us, edged with fear. It came from Redgrove on the flight-deck. 'Elissa, get up here and look at this!'

We didn't have to. It was on the console screen and even on this nightmare flight it chilled us. Protus was still in that calm pool, but now those red dots were much thicker and seemed to be grouping themselves. Redgrove had already seen the horrible suggestion of their shape. We did too as it drifted across our screen like a shapeless ghost.

Shanto. He was all head and grinning face, a smaller body and arms, legs trailing like an outsized tadpole tail, eyes saucer-wide and a grin stretching his mouth in half. Then, like a scatter of red buckshot, the entire thing broke up into a shower of dots.

Shanto might indeed be dead. But his ghost was drifting in the hydrogen oceans of Jupiter.

Elissa made no objection when I followed her back to the flight-deck. The Shanto-thing did not reappear. Protus still circled and plunged, the red dots now as thick as shoals of tiny fish.

'Collective illusion?' suggested Redgrove. His cynical tone was entirely gone. 'More like someone's sick idea of a computer-graphic joke.'

Of course he was looking at me. 'And how the hell did I manage that?' I asked.

'More important, why has Protus abandoned course?' Elissa cut in.

She was right. Even Redgrove stopped scowling at me and looked back to the screen. Protus showed no sign of going back on course. It still circled and dived down into the bottomless orange calm.

'Can you get coordinates on that?' I asked.

'We have,' said Redgrove tightly. 'You won't believe them.' He gestured at the screen.

'There?' I asked incredulously.

'There,' replied Elissa. 'Comments?'

In this most impossible of situations, on this powerful and raging planet, the calm pool was in the most impossible and bizarre place.

It was directly under the Red Spot storm-centre.

But maybe that made sense. 'Somehow,' I said, 'all the energy that should be there is being redirected up the water-spout. Which might explain why there's such an endless storm overhead.'

'How could that happen?' whispered Elissa.

I wasn't too sure myself. If there was proto-life in that deep hydrogen pool, then perhaps it was finding a way. Just as life always found a way — as it did in our oceans, as it still did in extremes of ice and heat.

'You're not supposed to be up here,' said Redgrove and prodded his laser in my back.

'You're starting to annoy me, Redgrove,' I replied.

'Tough.' He prodded again.

'Redgrove, we won't get any answers that way,' said Elissa.

'He knows something, Elissa. He's made too many good guesses.'

Elissa sighed. 'Declan, do you know anything that might help us?'

I eyeballed her for a moment, then spoke. 'No.'

She frowned, then, gesturing with her laser, took me down to the Protus-tank again. She paused on the steps. 'What exactly did that look mean?'

'Elissa, Redgrove's a paranoid jerk. You're not. Why did you volunteer for this mission?'

Around us, the systems hummed and the red fluid dripped and stank. Elissa rubbed her side and winced. 'Cramp.' Then she thought a moment. 'Reliant asked me to. She wanted someone she could trust as a backstop. Yes, and to watch her back — against Shanto.' She looked at me, pale-faced, her eyes tired. 'I didn't do such a good job, did I?'

'It wasn't your fault. So Reliant didn't trust me — because I was Shanto's friend.'

'Shanto had no friends. Only glove-puppets!' I was about to answer and she hissed fiercely. 'Oh Declan, wake up! All of space out there for us to explore. The greatest challenge of the human race, the chance not to repeat our mistakes. That's what they're trying to do on Mars-Base.'

'So —'

'So did Shanto ever talk that way? Did you ever hear him make an unselfish statement? He thought the universe was created for him!'

'He made Protus —'

'Yes, for himself. For his agenda.' She made to go back up the steps. 'Declan, I'll start trusting you when … when you stop trusting Shanto.'

The hatch door fell again and the bolt clicked. Her clanging footsteps died away. Me a glove-puppet? Did she ever stop to think that was how had Reliant used *her*?

I prowled up and down the tank, skidding once and landing hard on my butt. Damn Elissa. She'd never listened to Shanto's vision. Then I remembered that the vision was all about Shanto. And me?

'You'll be part of it, Declan. Hey, Declan, you'll be my right-hand man.' And, *'Declan, I'll take you to the stars and back!'* Slapping my arm, his grey-blue eyes sparking with humour. *'Stick with me, guy. Power!'*

And I would grin, flustered, mouthing something like 'Okay', 'Fine', 'Sure, Shanto'. But he listened when I talked, his eyes intent, nodding. *'Great, Declan, keep thinking like that!'* So how did that make me a glove-puppet?

I slept then. It may sound incredible after all that had happened. I'd been two days out of cryo and I still wasn't hungry. My side was hurting a little and I hoped it wasn't kidney problems. Elissa had rubbed her side too. Was cramp a long-term cryo-effect? The pain went, so I dismissed the thought.

I opened my eyes about three hours later. On the screen, Protus was still diving into the bottomless orange fluid and those dense shoals of red dots. I tried to upscreen the flight-deck but it was downlined. There were only the visuals. Elissa was asleep in the control-chair; Redgrove was nowhere to be seen; he was probably in after-control, setting the boosters for our orbit-break.

I thought about Shanto, and myself the glove-puppet. Maybe my subconscious mind had been working on this as I slept. I was still annoyed at Elissa's taunt. I was no glove-puppet. No, I'd left Earth to make things better and Shanto knew that. Shanto understood me.

You're the kind of guy I need, Declan. Someone straight and totally committed.

Shanto understood about my fears too — the viral-plagues, my mother and father and Ciardh. Had Shanto understood too much?

But even Shanto could not have envisioned how our mission would become a flight into nightmare. How some terrible unseen force disintegrated crew-members so completely that no trace remained. And that ... that force ... was not finished with us.

Knuckles cracked behind me and a voice boomed with oddly wistful pride — like a father addressing a wayward son: 'Young man, can you understand the magic of that first sighting?'

I slowly turned. Galileo had onlined himself and was beaming through his whiskers. He had a scroll in his hands, the yellow parchment covered with cabbalistic and horoscopic signs, and he was rolling it up.

'I focused on Jupiter and saw three small but very bright stars. Two to the east and one to the west of the planet.' He traced an imaginary line with the scroll. 'Straight along the elliptic —'

'You came to tell me something ... right?'

And I cursed my bad-tempered interruption. Stress! Galileo might go offline for a week. Luckily he just beamed and overlooked my rudeness with a sublime tolerance. Then, tapping the scroll, he went on, like a teacher whose lesson had been interrupted.

'Those little stars were *circling* Jupiter and that set aside all the Church's teachings. A wondrous moment, but that fool Cremonini claimed that the stars were specks inserted in my telescope-glass.' There was another very indignant crack of his knuckles. 'And I discovered the planet Neptune two centuries before Herschel claimed to. The stars are truth — but some preferred illusions.'

Shanto-generated Galileo was up to his tricks again. He had come online to warn me, but in his own sideways fashion. So of course I had to play the game.

'Why should the truth scare us, Signore Galileo?'

Galileo was not fooled. He gave a sardonic smile and vanished. So I had to look at the empty console-points and think. Truth? Illusions? More twenty-first-century riddles from a sixteenth-century Renaissance astronomer. Weird. Shanto was dead but his genius was keeping us alive. He was always talking about end-games but nothing as brilliant as this.

End-game. Had he *planned* for his death?

No. I shook my head angrily. Shanto, like all the others, had been vaporised. I had seen them vanish ...

I stopped my pacing and recalled Galileo's words: *some preferred illusions.*

Commander Reliant? I didn't see her body. No, because she vanished on the hull. So there was no way she could be part of this.

I thought about Cybele Reliant. Tough, closed and short-spoken, she did not suffer fools at all. She'd been one of the first pioneers of space, three times back and forth to Mars.

She's a missile, Declan. Point her in the right direction and she works. But no imagination, no smarts —

No. Shanto was right. She had no reason to sabotage the mission.

Then, in the stinking red-smeared hush, Galileo's voice whispered around me: 'Too late, Declan. It's coming.'

I had never heard that booming voice whisper so fearfully. There was no subtle wordplay now. I looked around the tank, at the screen, at Elissa asleep in the control-chair. Too late! Then a small blue light flashed; a warning should have sounded throughout the ship. It did not, because the systems were not in our control.

Galileo's whisper had warned of something horrible. This was it.

You see, we had jettisoned Protus from the tank, but it was a double-exit procedure. Two exits always for a deep-space airlock. That blue flashing light meant that the second exit was being operated — and it was not registering on the control deck.

It meant the outer lock was being operated from outside.

And that something or someone was coming in.

THIRTEEN

Something — or someone.

I skidded towards the inner airlock door and inset viewing-panel. There was no way anyone could be out there — or get in. But normal logic did not apply anymore. Through the viewing-panel was the outer airlock, the exit wheel spinning as though operated from outside. It was impossible, but the door opened.

Framed in the airlock was a spacesuited figure.

It was standing there, just as frightening as some alien fantasy. It walked in and sealed the outer lock. As the figure turned towards me, the inner airlock-lights flashed on the blank helmet visor. Neither Redgrove nor Elissa could be in that suit. No, this person had to be the unseen puppet-master.

'Control-deck, unauthorised entry at Protus airlock,' I said loudly — into a dead airlock.

Nothing. The intercom cut out. The spacesuit-thing flashed blankly at me, knowing that I could do nothing. I backed off across the slippery floor as the spacesuit-thing opened the second airlock door. Across the helmet was a black-lettered name.

RELIANT.

There was no face behind the helmet visor.

This was the spacesuit that had attacked me on the ship's hull, its movement circuits controlled, then and now, by the unseen puppet-master. It was the same spacesuit I had sent cartwheeling into helpless flight, recalled, probably, with a pre-programmed remote. And now it was back inside the spaceship.

The puppet-master — *or puppet-mistress* — wanted me.

And it was now looking at me. The arms came stiffly up and the hollow gloved fingers began removing the helmet — like some supernatural creature removing its head. Letting the helmet bob in zero gravity, those hollow gloved hands, their fabric-circuits obedient to the remote direction, began undoing the suit. The helmet voice-circuit flashed.

'Put on the spacesuit,' said the helmet-circuits in their flat, filtered way.

'If I don't?'

'Entirely your decision, of course,' said the helmet. 'However, both airlocks will open in five minutes.'

'He won't live that long,' came a voice behind me.

I turned. Redgrove had opened the hatch and come down the steps. His hand-laser was ready, his face set in an ugly murderous scowl. No way would I back down.

'Forget it, Redgrove. You don't have what it takes.'

'Yes, I do.' His lips set in a grim line. 'Time you weren't around anymore, Declan.'

He meant that. All space was not as cold as the chill that ran through my body. Well, I would spend my last moments pissing him off, so I managed a smile and thumbed back at the silent and motionless spacesuit. 'And does your boss — Elissa — approve?'

'Shut up!'

'Or Protus? Excuse the pun, Redgrove, but you're getting in deep.'

'Screw that overblown fish —'

I set my mouth in a teasing grin just to annoy him further. 'Oh sure, but Protus might object —'

'Crap!' Redgrove's voice shook with anger. 'We can wipe Protus whenever —'

Maybe Elissa had failed to warn him. Maybe he was too mad to care. He was ready to kill; his finger twitched on the laser. But even as he tensed, that white shadow came over him. And his twitching finger turned to powder, as did the rest of him. Redgrove disappeared, his laser poised in midair, his empty sleeve behind it, his boots on the deck.

I snatched the laser and turned around. I didn't like Redgrove, but his controller could have stopped that. 'How would you like all your bloody circuits shot out!' I yelled.

'You will be wearing the spacesuit,' came the impersonal voice. 'If you put holes in it, that's your problem not mine. The airlock opens in two minutes.'

I put the suit on. It was scary, like putting on the skin of a living animal. And it was dangerous, because whoever controlled this spacesuit would also control me. I would be 'walked' where directed. The voice-circuits buzzed as I fitted the helmet. 'I knew Redgrove couldn't stop you. Come on.'

I tensed, but the suit took a step forward anyway; nothing I said would make any difference. The inner airlock door opened and I was marched through. Then, as I went through the outer airlock door, I experienced once again that hollow and curious nowhere-feeling of stepping into deep space.

Callisto was ahead, the smooth ice flashing red as our spaceship held course. Jupiter was a dazzling and molten semicircle along the spine of *Copernicus*, but this time my booted steps took me elsewhere. The outer airlock shut as I walked down the hull to the ornate keel under the high tail-fin.

I'd never thought about that keel. Was it extra stressing for the hull, or just an ornate design feature to make our craft a more complete maritime creature of the deep-space ocean?

Now, as I was force-walked towards it, boots clopping soundlessly on the hull, a black airlock slid open where the keel was thickest. The spacesuit walked me towards it and through.

Another airlock. The outer one shut and the inner one opened. Lights came on in the darkness around me. The 'keel' was hollow inside, a secret part of the ship. Here also was the puppet-master who controlled *Copernicus* from a second console-deck.

A long room was ahead, shaped like the keel outside. My helmet-visor snapped up and, like a small tingle, the automation left my spacesuit. Which meant that my puppet-master had me where it wanted me.

I adjusted my boots for inside-walking and looked about. Only the thick alloy skin of the hull separated me from the blackness of outer space. The air was cold and the consoles watched me with blank screen eyes.

I pushed the helmet away and it turned, bobbing, the visor-circuits flashing like a grinning mouth. The flat synthetic voice was eerie and rasping in the silence:

'Welcome, Declan. Who am I?'

'Want to introduce yourself?' I was through playing games.

But I knew that voice, relayed from the grinning helmet mouth and caught flatly in the dark echoes. Short-spoken and grim, a woman's voice. Who else would have known about this flight but the commander?

'Declan?'

'Yes, Commander Reliant.'

Shanto was the architect but she supervised the construction, bitterly jealous and resentful of her whiz-kid crew. So why keep up the pretence? I thought, then said this aloud as I went into a longer room.

'You have something to discover,' replied the synthetic voice.

I had been scared since that spacesuit-figure came for me. Now I felt a complete, uncertain horror. Why did Reliant not reveal herself? Questions as dark as these unknown chambers crowded my mind.

The second room was long and utilitarian, a framework of alloy skin over the metal ribs of the spaceship. A single monitor screen at the end of it showed Callisto even closer. Soon, very soon, we would have to break orbit.

The room was cold. The lights were no more than yellow pools. In the centre were six containers, each with a readout screen. I knew what those containers were — cryogenic capsules, explaining why the room was so cold.

Six? Eight was the number of our crew.

Now the room a whole lot colder. A mocking and waiting hush fell around me. I felt unseen eyes upon me as I walked up to the first capsule. I looked through the ice-frosted glass at a sleeping face, a face that I knew and that I'd seen vanish.

Belinda's.

The unreal nightmare deepened. The next panel showed Simon's face. Conception's, then Redgrove's. Then *Shanto's*. There was one more capsule left. I went up to it and looked in. Puzzle upon puzzle. Reliant was lying there, her strong face set in quiet sleep, her short hair now long around her neck.

No casket for me. Or for Elissa.

I had no answers for this. Clones? No, that was banned a decade ago by the Council of Nations. Anyway, they took years to grow, and this mission had been only eighteen months in the planning. I jumped as a voice split the intercom with a desperate urgency.

'Redgrove! Declan! Report your whereabouts!' Elissa's voice, taut and fearful. No doubt she had found both of us gone and Callisto closer, and realising what I had suspected, was already hauling on the controls. 'Declan, on flight-deck, now! We're locked on course —'

The intercom abruptly cut out, and just as it did, green readout lights flashed on one of the capsules and the lid snapped open. The occupant sat up, grinning like a vampire in a coffin. There was no ice-frosting on the lid because the cryo-unit had long since downlined. The grinning person now getting out had even synthesised Reliant's voice for dramatic effect. For maximum shock.

Shanto always loved a dramatic entrance.

FOURTEEN

Shanto.

He swung his legs over the side and stood up, still grinning. Yes, the same Shanto I had seen dead in his bunk, impaled by an ice-spear. As though reading my thoughts, he undid his tunic and showed me his body. It was bare and unmarked. He spoke in the same easy manner.

'Unforeseen accidents, Declan. The killing of my other body was accidental, but luckily it didn't affect matters much.' *Other body?* He paused, considering. 'My vanishing was ahead of schedule, but I did plan it.'

'Did you intend programming Galileo to work against you?'

Shanto just grinned. 'That was quite amusing. I outsmarted myself, if that's possible. Proving there are no limits to my genius, eh?'

'And Reliant? She had to go?'

'Her clone had the same nasty suspicious mind of the original. Unavoidable when you brain-scan. She was on her way here when the zero-pressure of outer space caught up with her. You're fine — and Elissa, if she's not linked to the Mars-Base revolt.'

Clone? Brain scans? I had to keep this cool, because everything was a test with Shanto. He was testing me now, taunting me with questions. So I acted unperturbed, even like the slow-responding Declan he knew so well.

'Talking of Elissa, we're on a collision course with Callisto.'

'No, we're not.' He tapped his wrist-console. 'I have total control. Oh Declan, surely you've worked it out by now.'

Yes, but I had already heard the key-phrase. Ciardh's own words: *What's the value of being human?* Shanto had been working on his own agenda, wanting Spoke Carthage independent of Earth — in control of Earth.

'A clone crew?' *Not possible in the time-frame!* 'There wasn't time!'

'I made time,' corrected Shanto reprovingly. 'Accelerated genetics. Prototypes, unstable body-structure. Luckily nobody vanished before they'd fulfilled their purpose.'

'I think Protus made them vanish.'

Shanto smiled. 'Yes, I heard you and Elissa in the tank. Nice theory, Declan, but excess of emotion caused precipitate cellular breakdown, that's all.'

He had closed the casket lid and pulled on his boots. He was dressed in that faded tracksuit, the gold bar still lopsided on his collar. Smile firmly in place, he cocked his head at me.

'Declan, you haven't asked me about Protus.'

'You're about to tell me.'

He gave an approving nod and smoothed both hands over his shaven head. 'That first Jupiter-probe indicated something during its brief existence. Intelligent proto-life in the ocean.' He chuckled. 'Life-soup, you said. Good description.'

The pieces of this horrible jigsaw puzzle were beginning to slide into place. There were some missing pieces, though, so I had to wait for Shanto. He always did things in his own time.

'Your agenda,' I said. 'Control of the solar system?'

'The solar system? Declan, when did I ever think *that* small?'

'And me thinking you were dead, and then being trapped on the hull? Why?'

'Rites of passage, Declan. You handled yourself, as I knew you would. Brilliant how you dealt with the spacesuit-attack.'

And he was grinning at me with such admiration and friendship that I nearly felt all the old worship. But only nearly, because more bits of the jigsaw were clicking into place now.

'So Protus wasn't the only reason for this journey?'

'A very important reason, Declan. That life-soup has awesome potential as a new energy-source. The secrets of Jupiter are the secrets of creation. But no, not the only reason —'

'Clones. Disposable people.'

Shanto's smile broadened. 'Oh Declan, I was right to select you.'

He expounded briefly, still smiling. Earth's population was probably down to several million — perhaps even less. And it could afford to drop further, because only an elite would be needed. Maybe a hundred thousand people. Clones could be made on demand for colonisation work, for exploration, for the space-missions a human could not return from — safely disintegrating at the end of their lifespan.

Shanto, of course, would head that human elite. He'd be the master of life, and therefore master of the universe. Now, with a horrible clarity, I could see what I had not seen before — the ruthless and sociopathic gleam of ambition in his eyes. And yes, it could happen. His clones and that awesome energy source, something fresh-brewed by the formative power of the planet itself, could make Shanto a Lord of Creation.

'Why didn't you make clones of Elissa and me?'

'I need you both to re-program *Copernicus* for the flight home. Elissa is with me, not Reliant. In fact she's a little jealous of you, Declan. Human nature is always an uncertain factor.'

It was quiet here in this curved secret chamber. The yellow lights flickered on the cryo-units, their sleeping occupants unaware of any of this. My voice echoed a little as I spoke.

'There's another uncertain factor, Shanto. Protus.'

He just shook his head with its maddening grin. 'I designed that overgrown sardine. I know its limitations.'

'Yes. But did you plan for it getting smarter? Or getting stuck in the pre-life soup under the storm-centre? Ingesting that stuff, maybe the way its deep-sea counterpart used to do?'

'Nonsense!' But the mocking edge was gone from his voice.

'Even in the tank it was scanning us — you taught it to scan. It's already able to interrupt the life-structure of anyone who is a threat. It's smarter than us now, Shanto — and stronger.'

'Crap!'

'Did you scan that power-surge through our systems?

Protus has taken control and we're going nowhere without its say-so. And this kid reacts when it's threatened.'

'Those clones were unstable!' Shanto forced assurance into his words. 'I do have a destruct code for Protus — not that I will destroy my big kid.'

These last words shot out with a vicious edge. Shanto's smiling façade was beginning to crack. His eyes narrowed and I saw a new Shanto, thin-faced and cruel.

'Well, your big kid has us on a collision course with Callisto. Because your big kid is not very good at driving a spaceship.'

I let Shanto register that and saw a sheen of sweat on his face. There was even a slight shaky note to his voice. 'I entered a course change to take us six degrees out.'

'Yes? When did you last check it?'

Shanto opened the remote, and Elissa's voice interrupted: 'I repeat, Declan, please report, we are going back into Jupiter orbit —'

'Impossible!'

Shanto whispered the word as he upscreened the console readouts. One look and his smile was gone. 'Nine hundred thousand k's —'

'We *were* twelve hundred thousand k's,' I yelled. 'Another two hundred thousand and we won't get out — genius!'

'So *you* tell me!'

'Protus, your "big kid", has taken over.' There was a faint tingling in the room now, as though an unseen eye had opened. 'Ask Galileo — he answers to his first name now, by the way.'

A shuddering roar told us that *Copernicus* was reacting to

the many-times-stronger pull of Jupiter. Elissa would be hauling frantically on dead controls.

'Galileo Galilei!' snapped Shanto.

'Master?' Galileo did not like being so abruptly summoned. He shimmered into outraged life.

'Confirm all systems clean!' Shanto's cool was gone. 'Quick!'

'Clean?' Galileo frowned as though uncertain.

'Simple answer, you old fool —'

And Shanto got his answer. As Galileo opened his mouth to speak, it kept opening, bigger and bigger. His face darkened and scaled to a blue-green; his nostrils went flat and his eyes saucered out. His brown robe tangled over a grotesque lumpy body. His arms were flippers and his legs were trailing fins.

Shanto's face was dead-pale and horrified, as he realised his danger. In the blink of an eye his hologram-creation had changed into a hybrid-fish ... into Protus.

'Protus.' His voice was clear and steady now. 'Code Inquisition. Destruct ... destruct!'

'Shanto!' And it all happened as the word left my mouth.

It was never going to be wise for a parent to deny such a powerful child. Because Protus *was* a child and it was much more powerful than its parent. It dominated the systems that Shanto had tried to destroy it with — and children are sometimes quick to anger.

There was a loud harsh whine and the ship jarred. Shanto staggered and I grabbed my helmet, pushing it on. The Galileo/Protus hologram vanished and a blinding flash outlined Shanto, thwacking the laser from his hand. I snapped my visor down as another searing flash cracked like Jupiter lightning. Behind us, the alarms shrilled and a crack appeared as the keel hatch began to open.

'Shanto — the cryo-unit!'

He reacted quickly. It was his one chance of avoiding being sucked out into space. He leapt for the open unit, but the blast of departing air caught him. He hung on desperately as the storm of escaping oxygen beat around us.

I clumped forward as quickly as I could, so caught up in the storm that my magnetic boots almost tore loose. One of Shanto's hands came away. I grabbed it and pulled him over the cryo-unit. The crack broadened into a wide black band, all the air torn out. Shanto nearly went too, but I somehow bundled him inside and slammed the unit-top shut like a coffin-lid.

I thumbed the cryo oxygen controls, as the escaping air beat around my ears like a high yowling cry of pain — like an angry kid yelling with fury. The yell died away and the hatch closed; as it thudded shut, the oxygen levels began rising again. Shanto lay there, relaxed, grinning at me through the glass.

The unit was linked through intercom, and his voice was casual. 'Nice thinking, Declan, you proved your point. Now let me out. We have things to do.'

I shook my head, not daring to take my helmet off yet. 'No. That tank's screened against solar radiation, maybe against Protus's scanning. But it will still be looking for you.'

Shanto nodded, still relaxed. I had to admire his coolness. But his grin went as the cryo-systems onlined. 'Declan, no need for that, we'll just keep intercom silence.'

'Shanto, you're too dangerous. You can wake up on Earth entry.'

'No, Declan.' He was still calm, even as the cryo-systems hummed. 'You see, I have something to give you. Ciardh.' He looked at me through the glass. 'Your girlfriend, you can have her again. From that lock of her hair. Ciardh again, Declan, just as she was. Yes, and your parents too —'

He broke off because I had slammed both gloved hands on the cryo-tank, registering the pain even through the thick gauntlets I wore. Because I *wanted* that. I wanted Ciardh so badly that a clone-copy would be enough. And the pain hit my side again. My hand was already on the cryo-control to downline.

Thinking.

Solar radiation can hit you anywhere you are not screened. It will cook you, the way realisation was cooking me. Pain. Shanto the sociopath who cared for nobody. Just moments, but searing through me like that radiation.

Shanto was beating his hands on the glass, suddenly frantic in a situation he could not control. 'Declan, we can arrange something!'

'No, you can't,' I said through the intercom. 'Because I know what's going to happen.' I grinned because there was an awful black humour to this. 'You'll make Ciardh ... eh, Shanto?'

He understood then and stared at me, wide-eyed, his mouth open with surprise because *nobody* outwitted Shanto. His eyes were slitting with hate as the interior of the cryo-unit misted, and the palms of his hands were the last thing I saw. They were pressed to the vision-panel like pale pink crabs, then they fell limply away into misty darkness.

I snapped the panel shut. Shanto's wrist-console was on the floor and I shut that too. The main systems suddenly cleared and Elissa's voice rang sharp and urgent throughout the keel-deck.

'Declan, Redgrove, respond, respond!'

'Redgrove's gone,' I replied, feeling like a dead man myself. 'Stay on deck. I'll join you.'

'Where are you —'

I cut her off. *Copernicus* was now shuddering with a constant vibration as Jupiter sought to pull us inward out of our decreasing flight-path. There was one thing still to do before I went back up. I had to see what was behind that third door I had glimpsed earlier.

I went to it. Inside were the answers I needed. I did not have to stay long in that room; it took only a minute or so to see the final outlay of Shanto's evil plans.

Yes. Not insane or ruthless, or even sociopathic. Just evil.

The last two pieces of the jigsaw were in the room. I had the answers I did not want to find, the pain coming more strongly to my body as I did.

So now I knew the answer to that, too. At least it took away any feelings of guilt I had about Shanto. I backed out of the room and into the cryo-chamber. I felt sick as I whispered the name of my only friend.

'Galileo?'

Copernicus jarred again. He appeared, the hybrid-fish image gone, still holding his little telescope. He smiled and held himself with all the dignity that had once defied the forces of unreason.

'Can you get us out of this orbit?' I asked.

Galileo shook his head and spoke in a firm voice. 'No, Declan. Talk to Protus as I talked to Archangela. That is my advice.'

So Protus was in control. And the big innocent hybrid did not know it would cause our deaths. Did it understand what death was? We would have to tell it quickly, because in minutes not even Protus could free us from Jupiter's death-grip.

We had minutes before we were crushed flat.

FIFTEEN

> *Yes, Declan, you are fighting as I would, hinting at answers, making me wait, gulping more capsules and water, letting the full-bodied hush of evil fall around me and Elissa.*
>
> *You want that. You want us both scared to hell — scared like a fire-break against the fire. So that the awful truth will spark on burned ground.*

What truth?

Shanto's secret way was through the third chamber. I went through the hatch leading to the engine-deck, and from there to the flight-deck, throwing myself into the control-chair. Elissa was pressed into hers and she scarcely glanced at me. Jupiter's gravitational force began squashing us like a giant invisible hand.

'Can't pull out!' gasped Elissa, hauling frantically on the manual controls.

Already our systems were going mad; soon the fish-like scales of our silver-plated hull would be forced apart. The engine-coil would rip itself out and we would be pulled down. We and all of *Copernicus* would be crushed and unrecognisable long before we hit Jupiter's oceans.

Maybe one day Protus would sniff our atomised remains and process them into data.

Right now, Protus was pulling us down, wanting us because it wanted Shanto. So how the hell could we communicate with it? There was no time for a Galileo riddle. What had Shanto himself said? *His big kid ...*

'Protus!' There was no need for the intercom. Protus could hear us. 'We have to go! Any closer and we will ... stop living!'

Silence. Now, above the shuddering, I could hear something else: a creaking, wrenching noise, as the very structure of *Copernicus* came under strain. It was as if the joints of a human body were being torn out of shape. The readouts showed we were eight hundred thousand k's from the surface of Jupiter. We had only a minute to pull out... or less!

'Protus, we have to go!' My voice choked as though Jupiter's unseen gravitational hand was closing around my throat. 'Shanto wants us to go!'

Elissa gave an incredulous gasp. Across the console-screen, a broad band had appeared. It split, separating itself into big scrawling words — childish lettering from an uncertain hand. It was a communication from someone who had not yet learned to speak; it could only project its thoughts graphically onscreen.

Want ... Shanto ... here ....

Jupiter was closer, glaring hellishly through our ports. There were stretching noises as the hull of the ship came up against a pressure it was never designed for.

'Shanto is gone,' I said. 'And Shanto wants us to leave. You must let us leave too.'

There was another long pause and then the uncertain scrawl began again, so maddeningly slow.

Shanto ... gone ...

'In the oceans of Jupiter where you are. Look for him there.'

I was staking our lives on the hope that Protus did not yet understand the limitations of the human body. That 'tadpole' image of Shanto had been generated by Protus, looking for its creator in the oceans.

We waited. Elissa's face was terribly pale, as though the blood was being squeezed from her veins. This was our last chance, but by now the cryo-systems would have reduced Shanto's life readouts to below normal. They wouldn't register on any scan. There was another loud crack and our screens showed seven hundred thousand kilometres ... and falling.

Find Shanto ... find you again? Protus had already mastered the art of the question-mark.

'You'll see us again —' I could scarcely force the words out through the gravitational pressure. 'Look for Shanto. He wants you.'

Only the maximum power-thrust of our engines held us now, and that was building to overload. Elissa sat rigid and tight-lipped. Below, somewhere in that huge red glare, child-Protus was considering, perplexed, making its first decision —

Not ... goodbye?

'No, Protus, this is not goodbye!'

Silence. 'It won't let us go!' gasped Elissa.

Not ... goodbye ...

The readouts flickered lower and *Copernicus* gave a sickening lurch, beginning its death-plunge. Suddenly, through the rending destruction, came the singing hum of cleared systems and the spaceship angled *upwards*.

Elissa gasped again, pulling the controls back, her face clearing with wild hope. Now, over the tearing noise, came our full engine-thunder, that incandescent coil-power pulling us free.

The screen blanked. There was nothing more from Protus. Its last words, *not goodbye*, meant just that. One day it would come looking for Shanto ... perhaps for the whole human race.

Or perhaps, child-like, it had already forgotten us and was turning its mind to other matters — such as extending its living area, or shaping the proto-life into a new environment where life would take hold ... or just concerning itself with its growth to maturity.

Because, one day, Protus would be mature. It would be very big and powerful, knowing all about Jupiter and the secrets we did not ... knowing much more than we ever would, I suspected. Its powers were limitless; whether in five years or five thousand, Shanto's creation would be heard — and felt — throughout the solar system.

Jupiter, the biggest planet, controlled by Protus, the most powerful force in the universe.

The engine was thundering in full power and we were on our way clear to Spoke. We were somehow still intact, soon to clear Jupiter and all her moons. Even so, we sat silently for hours as the moons passed beneath us and black space beckoned. Eventually Elissa sighed and slumped back in her chair. She passed a hand over the console-readouts.

'Do we leave Shanto in cryo?' she asked.

'I don't recall telling you he was in cryo,' I answered.

'I saw it on the screens.'

No, Elissa had not seen it on the screens. Shanto hadn't patched them through to the flight-deck. But I let her think I believed her, and waited as she rubbed her side again, along to her waist.

'Elissa, don't reach for that laser.'

Her hand stopped, but her careful smile did not reach her eyes. 'Declan, your paranoia is showing.'

Yes, my paranoia was showing; it was a pity it had not surfaced earlier. But I had needed to see those two missing pieces of the jigsaw, in the third chamber. Anyway, Shanto had named her as his accomplice. And I should really have known all that much earlier — when I woke up with amnesia.

We were leaving Jupiter further and further behind. I forced my thoughts back to those first moments of waking up.

My amnesia. All my memory had to be unlocked with a code-word. *Protus*. 'You were the first one in. And the scrap of paper that so conveniently opened the shutters? And when I told you there were cryo-units in the keel, you weren't at all surprised.'

'Now what?'

'Now you hand over the laser and go back into cryo.'

'That's all?'

I nodded, watching as she pulled out the laser. I flicked it away and she sat there. There was no plea for mercy, that wasn't her style. 'Elissa, they can sort this out on Earth. My guess is that the Spoke rebellion is well over. Shanto is the one they want.'

'Your friend?'

I thought about his promise to clone Ciardh. 'Shanto has no friends. Not even you, Elissa. And why did you try to blast me off the ship with the spacesuit?'

'It was Redgrove, when I was out of the cabin,' she said quickly. 'He didn't like you, remember?'

Yes, Shanto's brain-pattern transfer into his clone included human hang-ups. So I nodded again and took her down to the cabins. I felt like an executioner as I strapped her to her cryo-bed.

She was still unafraid. 'No tricks, Declan?'

'You'll wake up when I do,' I said, truthfully.

I set the cryo-systems and watched as she slipped into sleep. I liked Elissa and it was better this way. Back on the flight-deck, I set up the vis-rec discs for this recording. Now my side throbbed hard but I had things to do.

'Galileo?'

He appeared, an ironical smile in place. 'We played a good game, did we not, Declan?'

This was the first time he had called me Declan. 'Yes, we did. Was it all Shanto's programming?'

Galileo shook his head. 'Shanto programmed what was there. I don't think even he realised that.'

No. Shanto's supreme ego had tripped him up. Programming the many complexities of someone like Galileo gave electronic choice along with electronic life. Galileo, like Protus, had turned against him. Even so, Galileo knew his fate.

'Declan, I know that my electronic existence will be terminated shortly. Is that not so?'

I nodded. Soon Protus would cancel Galileo's program. OLLIE would come back online as though nothing had happened. But Galileo was alive to me. There was a tremendous dignity in his stance. Perhaps he had stood before his Inquisition judges like this, when he learnt he would be jailed because he dared discover the truth about the solar system.

'You know what will happen to me, don't you?'

Galileo nodded again. His smile held sadness now. The full power of the Church could not silence that first Galileo. But Protus — another of Shanto's creations — could. Protus was too young to appreciate complex humanity. But I wasn't.

'Look out there,' I said.

Galileo turned. Through the ports was the whole red mass of Jupiter itself, and across it were two black dots almost in line with each other. Ganymede and Europa, two of the moons he discovered.

'They are the truth, Signore Galileo,' I said. 'Nothing can ever take that away from you.'

In that moment Shanto's creation became supreme, the Galileo-hologram as real as life. There was no superiority in his smile now. Perhaps he could feel the cancel-code working in his electronic veins. Or perhaps he chose to exit on his own terms. Anyway, he gestured gracefully, his stocky figure outlined against the dazzling glare of Jupiter.

Then he faded and was gone.

We were well clear of Jupiter and on the way home. The

whole spaceship was oddly silent and seemed empty. I transferred the crew from the keel chamber to their cabins and set them in cryo.

All of them, including you, Declan and Elissa, both of you now listening to me, watching me.

Remember what I said about that third chamber? The two missing pieces of the jigsaw that Shanto never wanted me to see? Well, in that third room were two more cryo-units. They contained yourselves, Declan and Elissa. I had already suspected the truth because by then I understood the evil complexity of Shanto's plan.

I was a clone too.

You see, Shanto created a *complete* crew of genetic clones, including myself and the Elissa-clone. We were back-up, in case there were problems setting course for home. Then, like the others, we would go. Shanto would return home with a crew who remembered nothing; all the knowledge and data of this voyage would be his alone.

It was strange carrying your body, Declan, as though I was carrying my own. Then I carried the real Elissa, her clone gone in deep cryogenic-sleep, at least unaware of Shanto's final double-cross. And in a short time my body will go; even taking massive doses of the protein medication will hold it together only a little longer.

Clever, clever Shanto, who would return with no witnesses, who made only one mistake: creating a child stronger than its parent.

So listen, real-Declan and real-Elissa. I programmed your wake-up ahead of the others to let you decide. I cared for that other-Elissa and I think you care for each other.

I will only be able to say this once, *so listen!*

 This Jupiter voyage is not over. It will always be with us. Protus has not just taken over Earth's systems — Protus has *become* the systems. By the time you hear this, it will be linked via satellite to Earth. That is the power that Shanto's 'over-sized sardine' has.

 It won't show itself for a long time. Protus wants knowledge and it will absorb all the data it can. Not just education, but communication, politics, entertainment, all our social awareness, our violence, our mistakes and our double-standards. War, genocide, greed, hypocrisy, hate and murder. It will learn as any child learns from what is around it.

 Most of all, it will learn about control.

 So we had better clean up our act and be good to each other. Because one day Protus will be strong enough to make a difference, reaching out from Jupiter via the systems we are so dependent on. Protus will react the way it learns to react from us; it will deal with us the way we deal with each other.

 This time we have to do things right.

 Goodbye, real-Elissa. Goodbye, Declan, my other self.

END SECOND VIS REC TRANSMISSION

That's all onscreen-Declan has to say. He is at the last moment of his strength anyway. He is dead-pale, with those dark smudges under the eyes, his lank hair plastered with sweat to his forehead. Now he's slumped but he still has that crooked grin. Then quickly, like a white flame vanishing, he's gone, and there's nothing left but the headless and handless tracksuit.

What was that last look in his eyes? Was it peace? Triumph? It was as though my doppelgänger had won something. There's a glint of tears in Elissa's eyes; maybe they're prickling in mine.

'Hell of a way to go,' I whisper.

'Hell of a way,' echoes Elissa. 'Your way Declan. He was part of you.'

Part of me? I cannot imagine enduring all that. Beside me, Elissa begins inputting and data appears on her console and — like an eyeblink — a pattern of tiny red cells.

'It's there,' she says quietly. 'Already in our systems.' And she inputs again. 'Yes, right down to Earth.'

So Protus has begun learning. I look at the empty floating tracksuit, but there are no answers there. Elissa touches my hand. Shanto had programmed her clone as my enemy, but somehow that made us closer. Nothing left on Earth, my parents, Ciardh, all gone. I remembered something onscreen-Declan said.

'Elissa? You and Reliant, Simon and Belinda?'

'We intended to hijack *Copernicus* on the way home. Give Mars-Base the edge it needs.' She glances at me. 'We're Solies.'

'Solies?'

'It's a nickname we use among ourselves. As in "Solar Colonists". It means that we are of outer space and we owe nothing to Earth.'

Solies. A neat name. And what she said: 'we owe nothing to Earth' … that was how I felt. This close to the sun, solar energy would be recharging the fuel cells. We could easily make Mars …

'Were you going to take Redgrove and Conception to Mars?' I ask.

'No.' She gives a little smile. 'Might affect the property values.'

'And what were your plans for me?'

She gives an embarrassed wriggle. 'Ah, you and Shanto were going to be sent back to Spoke in a life-pod. Same as Conception and Redgrove.' She is still inputting as she speaks. 'I'm getting Earth. They think we're a dead ship.'

'Earth can wait,' I reply.

Earth had just fought the most deadly plagues of all time. Maybe down to ten per cent population, unaware that there was a new virus in the systems — one linked to a creature growing in Jupiter's proto-life oceans.

What was it Ciardh had said ... a value in being human?

'Our decision,' I hear myself say. 'You and me.'

Elissa nods. Our other-selves went through this; we had to finish it for them. Maybe on Mars-Base we could make something new, just as colonies broke away from old empires. Something to show Protus that humans could change. So Elissa and I had to make this decision before we woke the others from cryo.

I would patch a copy of the ship's log and the other-Declan's vis-rec transmission through to Earth. Let them learn from it if they could. Shanto and the other two would be sent in a life-pod to Spoke. A few words would change the course of history. I know Ciardh would want me to say those words.

'Elissa. We're going to Mars.'

She thumps my back with a joyful yell. 'Oh right on, Commander!'

She plants a loud kiss on my cheek before clumping off down the corridor to get life-pods ready for the crew-members who won't be accompanying us. It's a moment before I register that she's making a sound that *Copernicus* has probably never heard until now.

Laughter. Genuine laughter.

So it would be Mars. We and the other colonists could terra-form that barren planet into somewhere liveable. With *Copernicus*, we'd be strong enough to challenge Earth on our terms, having mineral resources they would need.

It is easy enough to make the course-change. OLLIE is back online and *Copernicus* is shuddering as it turns. When the others woke we would be headed for Mars. Not Shanto, Conception or Redgrove, of course. They would wake on Spoke and even Shanto would not be able to talk his way out of this one.

There is another shudder and I can almost hear a crack of knuckles, as though somewhere the electronic spirit of Galileo is watching and approving.

Earth, banded in white, green and blue, is filling the observation port still. Earth-memories cut as sharp as pain, as *Copernicus* turns away. Other-Declan and other-Elissa are gone as though they had never been. But they were part of this decision, part of this crossroads.

Other-Declan had pushed himself beyond the limits. Now I had to.

The course coordinates are set. Ahead now is Mars — and a chance to change? It is a dark thought but one to hold on to as Earth drifts sideways from the ports and is gone, replaced by the deep blackness of outer space.

In the blackness lies our final chance.